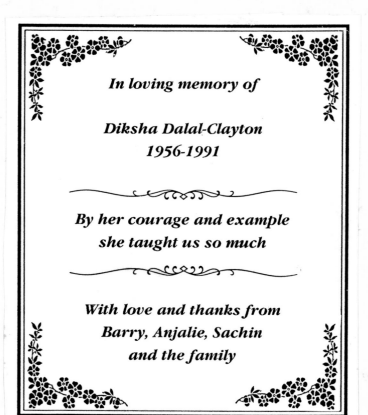

In loving memory of

Diksha Dalal-Clayton
1956-1991

By her courage and example
she taught us so much

With love and thanks from
Barry, Anjalie, Sachin
and the family

The Adventures of Young Krishna
The Blue God Of India

THE ADVENTURES OF YOUNG KRISHNA
KRISHNA
The Blue God Of India

Diksha Dalal-Clayton

THE LUTTERWORTH PRESS

CAMBRIDGE

The Lutterworth Press
P.O. Box 60
Cambridge CB1 2NT

British Library Cataloguing in Publication Data
Dalal-Clayton, Diksha
The adventures of young Krishna; The blue god of India
I. Title
398.210954

ISBN 0-7188-2839-9

Illustrations by Marilyn Heeger

Printed in Great Britain at the University Press, Cambridge

Dedication

For Krishna; for my children, Anjalie and Sachin; and for my widely scattered family.

    With love and thanks.

Diksha Dalal-Clayton
April 1991

Diksha passed away on 8 June 1991 after a long and courageous fight against cancer. The family and the publishers have worked together closely to ensure publication of this collection of stories about Krishna, as a tribute to Diksha's memory and to her many talents.

    May she rest in peace.

Whenever his friends grew tired of playing their games, they would settle down around Krishna and listen to his music.

Contents

KRISHNA - THE BLUE GOD OF INDIA

Stories about Krishna are told wherever you go in India, from the high Himalayan mountains of the north, to the hot, shimmering jungles in the south.

In India, people believe that whenever things are badly wrong in the world, a very brave and special person is born on Earth to fight evil and help the good. They believe that such people are the human form of God, or incarnations of God.

This is why Krishna was born in India a long, long time ago, before our grandparents or even their grandparents were born. He was so brave and strong and handsome that people have told stories about his life for hundreds of years.

Everyone loves Krishna, especially children, because although he was a god and did things that no ordinary person could do, he also behaved like any other child. He was good and bad, just like all of us. Children like to hear the stories of his adventures because he fought demons and monsters of all kinds, and always won. Yet, even though he was always brave and fought for good causes, Krishna himself was not always good in the way that adults expect children to be good.

INTRODUCTION

We were a large family with uncles, aunts, cousins and grandparents coming and going and sometimes all staying under one roof. All the children ate and played and fought together, and there were times when the noise was just too much for the adults.

The only thing that was guaranteed to keep all the children quiet was the promise of stories. We had no television and few books, but there was usually a grandmother, an aunt or a mother who was willing to sit down and tell us stories.

Of course, there was a price to be paid. I remember having very mixed feelings whenever I saw those huge sacks of rice and lentils and spices lined up against the back door, for I knew there would be no hopscotch, no marbles and no climbing trees that day. Instead, we girls would have to sit cross-legged on the veranda floor with large, round trays on our laps filled with whatever it was, picking out the sticks and stones, sifting and cleaning. This was our contribution to the daily round of cooking for and feeding so many people. It was a boring and fiddly job which I hated, and the only thing that ever made it worthwhile for me was the prospect of stories. Stories about Ancient India, of magic and miracles, Ram and Sita, Radha and Krishna.

It made no difference to me that I was sitting in the middle of Africa, as far as I could possibly be from that mythical, mystical land. For me it was a land of Maharajahs and Ranis, of monsters and Rakshasas, sadhus and saints. The quiet voices of my grandmother, my aunt or my mother told us the stories just as they had heard them when they were children. They painted vivid, technicolour pictures in my mind which are as sharp today as they were when I was little.

I loved stories about Krishna. It was comforting to know that there was a god who knew what it was like to be constantly in trouble.

If a god could steal butter and still be good, there was hope for me. The idea that his skin was blue fascinated me too: It was so much more interesting than my own drab brown, and the thought that Krishna could be such a strange colour, and lie and steal and still get away with it, was wonderful.

Krishna's life was lived on a grand scale. Everything was larger than life, and our own day to day grumbles were petty compared to the calamities which befell the people in the stories. Rage and jealousy and evil all played their part, but it was balanced by good, and reassuringly the good always won.

It was through the stories we heard while chopping vegetables for the next meal, or sifting chapati flour, or doing other tedious jobs that we began to understand the meaning of our Hindu festivals and customs. It was through following the lives of the people and the gods and goddesses in those stories that we came to understand the importance of duty and responsibility towards our family, and everything that we knew to be good. The stories gave us a framework around which to shape our lives. They showed us the difference between good and evil, and although we didn't know it at the time, the lessons we learnt seeped naturally and easily into our minds and stayed there.

Of course we read stories in English at school, but the world they created in my mind was dull and foreign. The rhythm and the beauty and the magic were not there, and it was only when I learnt about the Greek and Roman gods and goddesses that I began to understand what I had been missing. The Greek and Roman myths captured the same feeling of mystery which I felt when I heard the stories about Krishna, Ram, and the other Indian gods and goddesses.

The world is different now. Not many families live together as ours did when I was little, and children are lucky if they have someone on hand who will tell them the stories that they themselves heard when they were small. It would be a pity if we lost the magic of those ancient stories forever, never to be heard again.

I hope that this collection of stories will colour the imaginations of those who have not had the chance to enjoy them before.

LIST OF INDIAN WORDS

Ayah   A nanny or nurse.

Ashram   A school, usually run by a religious teacher.

Bhagwaan   God.

Brahmin   A priest, or a person from the priestly caste.

Banyan tree   A shady tree, whose branches can take root
                to form new trees.

Chapati   Another word for Roti, a type of flat, round bread
                eaten in India.

Frangipani   A tree with very sweet-smelling white, pink or
                yellow flowers.

Ghee   Clarified butter, boiled to remove impurities.

Gopi   A milkmaid.

Gullies   Ravines.

Hookah   A kind of smoking pipe where the smoke is sucked
                down a tube through water to cool it.

Jasmine   A shrub with sweet-smelling white or yellow flowers
                which are smaller than frangipani flowers.

Kohl   Black eye make-up.

Ladoos   Round, crumbly sweets, about the size of a child's
                fist, made from flour or semolina and ghee, nuts,
                sugar and spices.

Lotus   A flowering plant which grows in water, a type of
                water-lily.

Maharajah	A King or Prince, ruler of a state.
Monsoon	Seasonal tropical rains.
Muni	A religious teacher.
Mahut	An elephant trainer.
Mango	The fruit of the mango tree, which when unripe is green and hard. When ripe, the skin of a mango turns yellow or red, and its flesh becomes juicy and a deep orange colour.
Mantra	A magic spell, or sacred words repeated in prayer.
Peepul tree	A sacred tree rather like the Banyan.
Parakeet	A type of small, long-tailed parrot.
Rajah	A ruler or lord of an estate, not as important as a Maharajah. ('Maha' means 'great'.)
Raas	A type of dance, usually in circle formation, in which the men and the women each use a pair of arm- length sticks to beat the rhythm.
Rakshasa	A demon.
Sari	A very long piece of cloth wound round the body and worn as a kind of dress by Indian women.
Sandalwood	An evergreen tree with scented wood.
Sadhu	A Hindu holy man.
Scythe	A tool with a long, thin, curved blade used for cutting crops.
Talwaar	A type of heavy sword, with a long, curved blade.
Thali	A round metal plate, similar to a tray.
Tulsi	A herb, a type of basil considered sacred by Hindus.

LIST OF INDIAN GODS AND GODDESSES

Bhagwaan	God, the Almighty.
Brahma	The first being to be created, and the creator of the universe. One of the Hindu Trinity.
Indra	The King of Heaven.
Krishna	Also known as Kahna, Govinda and Gopala. Incarnation of Vishnu.
Lakshmi	The goddess of wealth.
Prithvi	The Earth goddess.
Shiva	The Destroyer. Another of the Hindu Trinity.
Surya	The Sun god.
Vishnu	The Preserver. The third of the Hindu Trinity.
Yama	Lord of the Dead.

RAKSHASAS (Demons)

Aghasura	The demon who turned into a python and tried to swallow Krishna and his friends.
Bakasura	The demon who turned into a giant stork and tried to kill Krishna.
Putna	The demon who tried to kill Krishna with her poisoned milk.
Vatasura	The demon who turned into a bull and tried to kill Krishna.

Devaki was holding the baby in her arms, cuddling and soothing her.

KRISHNA IS BORN

Once upon a time, when India was a land of magic and maharajahs, there was a little kingdom on the banks of the Yamuna River. Every spring the fast-flowing waters of this river in northern India were fed by the melting Himalayan snow. The land all around the Yamuna was lush and green, rich and fertile. The people of Mathura farmed, traded and prospered; and every year they made sacrifices to thank the gods for their good fortune.

Life would have been perfect for these good and hard-working people had it not been for their King. The Maharajah of Mathura, whose name was Kans, was known far and wide as a monster. When he was young, he had wanted to be King so much that he was prepared to do anything. Rather than wait, as a dutiful son should, to inherit the throne, he plotted to overthrow his father so that he could be King instead. The citizens of Mathura were terrified of Kans because he did exactly as he pleased, often killing or imprisoning people just because he didn't like them.

Kans' father Ugrasen had always been kind and just to his people, whilst Kans had never shown them any kindness even as a young boy. He had always behaved as if it was his right to walk into any house or shop and demand whatever he wanted. He pestered girls from respectable families and when their parents hid them away, he had their homes destroyed. For a while the people of Mathura had felt powerless to do anything. Finally, things became so bad that a group of merchants decided to complain.

The old King of Mathura regularly held court at his palace where he listened to complaints, resolved quarrels and generally helped his people in whatever way he could. At these courts, even the most humble street-sweeper knew that he would be listened to with

1

respect, and that he could speak freely without fear of punishment. The merchants decided that this court was the place to make their complaint. As usual, the courtroom was full of people. There was hardly room to stand. The merchants waited for their turn to speak, and when it came, they all stood up together. They were trembling and wringing their hands nervously. They knew that their King was a fair and just man, but what would he do when he heard complaints against his own son?

The King saw at once that the merchants were afraid and he spoke to them kindly.

'Speak freely, my good merchants,' he said. 'Tell me what is worrying you. A King is a father to his people, and like a good father, I am here to listen to your problems, whatever they may be.'

At this, the merchants felt more confident, and their leader began to speak.

'Sire, you are indeed like a father to us. We love you as a son loves his father, and we have always felt that we could come to you whenever we have needed help and advice, but...'

'Speak, my dear man, speak,' said the old King graciously.

'Well, Sire, it's about Prince Kans,' said the merchant. 'We have tried to be understanding and we don't mind giving him presents, but, Sire, we are not rich, and now even our daughters are not safe...'

Ugrasen didn't need to hear any more. This was just what he had always suspected. He had tried to teach his son how to behave by setting a good example, but now he knew that he had failed. Even the wise men who had taught Kans as a boy had not been able to control his mean and cruel nature. The old man shook his head and sighed sadly. He was ashamed to hear his subjects complaining about his own son, but in all fairness, he knew that they would not have complained without proper cause.

'I have heard your complaint and I promise you that my son Kans will not bother you or your daughters again,' he said. 'Court dismissed.'

The King left the courtroom and ordered his sentries to bring Kans to him at once. He began pacing the floor impatiently but before long he heard footsteps tramping down the passage. The door flew open and Kans marched in, followed by the sentries. Every man had his sword drawn and pointed at the old King.

'What is the meaning of this?' demanded Ugrasen.

'Can't you guess, Father?' sneered Kans. 'It means that these men are under my orders and they will do as I tell them.' He turned to the sentries. 'Take him away to the dungeons, and make sure that I never see him again!' he ordered.

The awful news of what Kans had done soon spread throughout the little kingdom. It was the worst thing that could have happened to the people of Mathura. They had dared to complain about Kans, and now he was their King instead. From now on he had the power to make life twice as difficult for them.

It was just as they had predicted. Within days, Kans' soldiers were seen in every street. They looted shops and houses and threatened innocent people. His spies were everywhere. Any person heard complaining about Kans was immediately imprisoned or killed. People began to disappear never to return, and soon the very air in Mathura smelt of fear.

As the years went by Kans became more and more cruel, and although the people of Mathura were well fed and clothed, their life became a misery. They lived in constant fear and no-one could tell when Kans' evil eye would fall upon them. It seemed as though even the gods to whom they prayed every morning and evening had forsaken them.

The people of Mathura did not know it, but Prithvi, the Earth goddess, had been watching her people's suffering for some time. Her temples were filled with men and women begging for help. Each day, the temples echoed with the sound of their cries, which became more desperate as the days passed. Powerless to do anything by herself, Prithvi turned to the other gods and goddesses for help.

Up in the heavens above the highest mountains in the land, Indra, the King of Heaven, already knew about Kans' reign of terror. Hearing Prithvi's call, he summoned Brahma the Creator, Vishnu the Preserver and the Good, and Shiva the Destroyer of the Universe. Together they would surely be able to think of a plan to destroy Kans. Although they were gods, they could not meddle in the affairs of mortals on Earth unless they themselves took the form of mortals.

The gods decided that only Vishnu's powers of good could fight Kans' evil.

'Have faith,' said Indra to Prithvi. 'We know how the people of Mathura have suffered, and soon, a child will be born on Earth who will rid Mathura of its evil King.'

Reassured by Indra's words, Prithvi returned to Earth to wait for the coming of the miracle child.

Kans had a younger sister called Devaki who was different in every way from her brother. Devaki was a quiet and gentle princess who was as kind as Kans was cruel, and as humble as he was proud. When Devaki grew old enough to marry, Kans made sure that she would marry a man from outside Mathura. He wanted to make sure that if Devaki had sons, they would not be able to claim his throne from him. Devaki had been terrified of her brother all her young life, and she was happy enough at the thought of leaving Mathura forever. Kans was so pleased at the thought of ridding himself of his sister that he planned a very grand wedding indeed.

As dawn broke on the wedding day, the streets of Mathura were already decorated with streamers of mango leaves and sweet-smelling frangipani and jasmin flowers. Kans ordered his court musicians to play their loudest and most joyful music, and sent servants out into his kingdom to deliver sweets made of milk and ghee, honey and nuts to every family. Each woman was given a sari of glistening silk, and each man a shawl of the finest wool. By the time Devaki's bridegroom, whose name was Vasudev, arrived for the wedding, every face in Mathura was smiling.

Kans was beaming as he watched the priest chanting prayers over the holy fire. Devaki and Vasudev exchanged their marriage vows in front of the fire, which filled the air with the smell of burning sandalwood, ghee and incense. When they finally garlanded each other with flowers and knelt before the priest for his blessing, a tremendous cheer went up in the streets of Mathura. Now everyone knew that Vasudev and Devaki were man and wife.

It was while entertaining his guests at the wedding feast that one of Kans' most trusted servants came to him with a message.

'Sire,' he whispered into Kans' ear, 'there is an old man waiting to see you outside the palace gates. I have told him that you are too busy to see him today, but he refuses to go. He insists that what he has to say is a matter of the utmost importance to you. He says that he has come to warn you.'

'Who would presume to give me, the King, a warning?' wondered Kans. 'I know that people in Mathura hate me, but they wouldn't dare to harm me.' Nevertheless, he arranged to meet the man outside the city, away from curious eyes and ears. Kans had been enjoying himself at the feast, indulging his love of good food and drink, and he was not pleased to have to leave it. As he hurried to meet the man, Kans began to wonder if he was walking into a trap. He felt suspicious, and he was in a very bad mood by the time he reached the meeting-place.

The old man was sitting under a large peepul tree where he had been ordered to wait. He was sitting cross-legged, murmuring a prayer with his eyes closed. In his thin, wrinkled old hands he held a string of fragrant sandalwood prayer beads. As he prayed, he seemed to be counting the beads, picking at each one slowly.

Most people would have waited for the old man to finish his prayers but Kans was not used to being kept waiting. He was already irritated at having to leave the feast, and he marched up to the man.

'What do you want, old man?,' he demanded roughly. 'Tell me what you have to say and be off with you!'

'Gladly, Sire,' replied the old man confidently, 'but if I were you, I should show a little gratitude to a man who has come to warn you. You are happy today, are you not? You think that you are safe because your sister will soon leave for her husband's home far away. Beware! Beware! You have wronged many people, and your own sister's eighth child will kill you before you are as old as I am.' With that, the man bowed low and hobbled away.

At first Kans was astonished. Then he became frightened and angry. He was so wild with rage and fear that by the time he reached the palace again, he wanted to kill Devaki at once. The wedding guests began to leave. They were frightened at seeing Kans in such a terrible temper. Soon all but Vasudev's closest relatives had left, and even they were ordered out of the palace by Kans. When only Vasudev and Devaki remained, Kans unsheathed his talwaar, a mighty curved sword.

'You must die, Devaki,' he growled. 'A wise man has said that your eighth child will kill me, so I cannot let you live.'

When Vasudev heard this, he was so horrified that he threw himself at Kans' feet in despair.

'How can you believe the words of a strange, wandering beggar?' he cried. 'Please, I beg you, spare Devaki's life. It is not Devaki that you have been warned against, but her child. I promise on my life that I shall hand you all our children as soon as they are born, if only you will let Devaki live.'

Even Kans could see that a newborn baby could not kill a grown man. He felt that he could trust Vasudev to keep his word, so he agreed to let Devaki live. However, to make sure that they kept their promise, he decided to lock them both up in a prison cell in the palace. He posted guards outside the cell day and night, and Devaki and her husband began their life together in a small bare room, under lock and key.

As the years went by, Devaki and Vasudev grew to love each other more and more dearly, and each child that they lost to Kans made them more determined to save the next. By the time that their seventh child was about to be born, they had learnt that the only way to save their baby was to keep it quiet and try to hide it. Soon a baby girl was born to Devaki, but although they tried to hush her cries, one of the guards heard the child crying and ran to tell the King. Kans hurried to the cell as soon as he was told about the baby. He had come to kill the child with his own hands as he had done all the others. Devaki cried and pleaded with her brother.

'How can this little babe hurt you, my brother?' she wept.

Kans roared angrily as he grabbed the infant from his sister's arms and threw her onto the stone floor. The baby glowed strangely as she fell, and when she hit the ground, she turned into a bolt of lightning which shot up towards heaven.

'You have too much blood on your hands to save you now, evil Kans,' she cried. 'Beware my brother, who will be born to destroy you!'

Devaki and Vasudev were as astonished as Kans and the guards, but if they expected any mercy they received none. Kans became even more determined that the eighth child should not be left alive. He doubled the guards at the prison door, arming them with swords and daggers, and he called a sorcerer to protect him with magic spells and potions. Devaki and Vasudev were as determined to protect their child as Kans was to slay it, and for the next year they prayed desperately every day.

The hot weather came and went, and clouds began gathering in the sky, growing heavier with moisture every day until soon they would pour rain onto the hot, dry land. People all over India were praying for the rains to come soon, because without rain their crops would fail and they would starve.

Krishna, Devaki's eighth child was born as the monsoon rains broke on a very stormy night. A thunderstorm was raging outside, lashing rain against the palace walls. The wind moaned and howled, blowing the trees back, and the Yamuna River became an angry, soaring torrent. All across the kingdom people tried to shelter from the storm wherever they could, and within the palace, the royal nannies, the ayahs, were busy trying to comfort frightened, crying children. All the rest, servants, sentries and courtiers were peering through the windows into the darkness, wondering at this sign of heavenly anger.

As Krishna was born, there was a sharp crack of thunder and a voice boomed across the skies.

'Vasudev, you must take this baby across the river to Gokul and exchange him for your sister's newborn girl. Never fear, your son will be saved. God is with you!'

Devaki and Vasudev realised at once that their prayers had been answered. But what if everyone else had heard the heavenly voice too? They were sure that Kans and his guards would try to stop Vasudev escaping with the baby. But when they looked around, they were amazed to see that the guards had dropped into a deep sleep exactly where they were standing, and the cell door had magically flown open. Devaki was heartbroken at the thought of losing this child too, so soon after his birth. She held him closely for a few moments, stroking his curly black hair. This child unlike all her other babies was unusually dark-skinned, looking almost blue at times.

However, it was time for Vasudev to leave, and Devaki watched tearfully as he wrapped the baby Krishna into whatever rags he could find. He put the little bundle into a basket and ran out of the prison and through the palace. No-one stopped him, for every man, woman and child in the palace was mysteriously asleep. Vasudev didn't stop to wonder at this sight and hurried towards the Yamuna River, hoping against hope that the ferryman had at least left his boat by the river bank.

It was only when he reached the river that he realised what a foolish hope it was. Even if a boat had been left out that night, it would have been smashed up and carried away by the fierce current. Vasudev decided that his only hope was to swim across the river. He looked up at the angry, crackling sky and called out as loudly as he could, 'I am in your hands, my Lord!'

He stepped into the foaming water, and as he did so, it parted to make a path across to the other side. The many-headed Shesha Nag, the Serpent King who lived in the river, reared up out of the water with its hood open over Krishna as if sheltering him from the storm. At first Vasudev thought that the snake was about to attack them, but he then realised that it was actually protecting Krishna.

Vasudev reached the other bank safely. It was still raining heavily, but he hurried to the village of Gokul where his sister Yashoda lived. Surprisingly the door to her house was unlocked, and as Vasudev entered he saw that Yashoda and her husband Nand were both fast asleep with their new daughter beside them. He crept up quietly, exchanged the babies, and quickly made his way back to the river with the baby girl.

It had stopped raining and the flood waters had subsided by the time Vasudev reached the river. He was able to swim across safely, pushing the baby in her basket in front of him as he swam. It was almost morning by the time Vasudev reached the palace in Mathura, and he was frightened that the guards would be awake and find him gone. He need not have worried because everyone in the palace, except Devaki, was still fast asleep when he reached the prison cell. The moment Vasudev was inside however, the locks clanged shut on the cell door. The noise woke the baby, and it started crying as new babies do.

The guards were stirring and the sounds of the usual hustle and bustle soon began to fill the palace. Kans had been waiting anxiously for news of the new baby and ran to the prison cell as soon as he was told of the child's cries. Devaki was holding the baby in her arms, cuddling and soothing her. She began to cry when she saw Kans, pleading for mercy. Kans ignored her pleas. He tore the baby away from his sister and was about to smash her to the ground, when the infant flew out of his arms.

'Kans, you wicked child-killer!' cried the baby. 'He who will destroy you is already born. God commands you to release Devaki and her husband, for you have nothing more to fear from them!' With that, the child vanished before their very eyes.

Kans was beside himself at being so easily tricked, and he threatened to kill Vasudev and Devaki at once. However, the guards and all the courtiers who heard what had happened realised that such an act would surely bring disaster upon them all. They begged Kans to spare his sister and her husband, reminding him that this was God's command. Kans finally agreed to let Devaki and Vasudev live, but he refused to set them free. He was so angry at being deceived, and so frightened for his own life, that he vowed to kill every baby boy in Mathura.

'I shall not rest until I have found and killed this horrible child!' he thundered.

Immediately, he ordered his soldiers to search all the houses in Mathura, and to kill every baby boy they found. Soon, mothers throughout the kingdom were in a panic trying to save their babies and their little boys from the soldiers. Kans did not rest until the only children left in Mathura were girls, and for days, all that could be heard in the kingdom were the cries of screaming children and weeping mothers.

If Krishna had been in Mathura he would surely have been killed, but for a while at least, he was safe. What Kans did not know was that the child he feared was being raised as the son of Nand and Yashoda in Gokul, which lay outside his kingdom.

Yashoda began to wind the rope round and round Krishna's little body but the tighter she wound it, the looser it seemed to get.

BUTTER THIEF

Gokul was a quiet and peaceful village where life revolved around cattle and the land. Farmers worked hard tilling their fertile land and tending their cattle. However, it was not a small village and there were other people who were in many ways as important to the smooth running of the village as the farmers. There were sweepers and shoemakers; potters who made clay pots for cooking and storing food; tailors to sew and mend clothes and washermen to wash them; and there were Brahmin priests in the temples to bless births and weddings. Nand and Yashoda's home was a safe and happy place for Krishna and their older son Balram to grow up in.

Every morning as the sky glowed pink in the east and the peacocks began calling, the women of Gokul hurried out into the cool air to milk their cows. Here, as in almost every village in India, men, women and especially children loved and respected cows for all the goodness which they gave people. In return for a little care every day, a cow gave milk which could be used for drinking or for making yoghurt, butter, buttermilk or ghee. As dawn broke each day, every woman's first job was to feed and milk her family's cows.

Krishna liked to be up early in the morning too, and often followed his mother Yashoda to the cowsheds. He liked to give the cows their baskets of seed and hay, stroking their warm flanks and singing to them gently as they munched their feed. If Krishna was lucky and there was enough milk, Yashoda would give him some straight out of the milking pot. He loved the fresh, warm milk so much that he was always disappointed when there wasn't enough spare for him to drink straight away. There was only one thing which he liked even more than fresh milk, and that was home-made butter. Krishna loved butter so much that he would do almost anything for it, and this constantly led him into trouble.

11

Unfortunately for Krishna, most families stored their butter in clay pots which they hung up high from the rafters, where even the slightest draught would cool the pots and keep the butter fresh. In Gokul, this was also the best way to keep it safe from Krishna's greedy hands. All the women had learned that if they left butter within Krishna's reach, not only would he steal it, but in his hurry to escape before he was caught, he quite often broke the pots too. Krishna soon learnt that he had to be quite clever if he didn't want to be caught stealing butter. Of course he knew very well that stealing was always wrong, but he could never quite control his craving for butter, and he was almost always caught.

Once, Krishna was caught stealing butter from his mother's butter pots which had been neatly stacked in a corner, ready to be hung. He had worked his way from one clay pot to another, and as he finished with each pot, he carefully replaced it so that no-one could tell that it had been disturbed. Krishna gorged himself until he could eat no more, and he was just about to sneak out of the room when he heard his mother's anklets jingling by the door. Krishna turned around and smiled, pretending that all he was doing was making sure that the pots were properly covered. Luckily, he had managed to lick every trace of butter from around his mouth, and for a moment he really thought that he had got away with his crime.

Krishna smiled so innocently that Yashoda almost felt guilty about suspecting him. And yet, whenever it was particularly quiet in the house, she knew that Krishna was up to some mischief. Finding him in the butter-room was definitely not a good sign, but none of the pots looked as if they had been tampered with.

'Come on, Krishna, out you get,' she said firmly. 'You know very well I don't like you playing around the butter pots.'

Krishna rushed past Yashoda at once, relieved that he had escaped so easily. He was just beginning to think he was clear when he felt his mother's hand closing around his arm.

'You're in quite a hurry to get away, aren't you?' said Yashoda quietly. 'Are you sure you haven't been stealing any butter?'

'Oh no, Mother,' said Krishna quickly. 'Does it look as if I have?'

'That's not the point,' his mother said, even more suspicious now. 'Open your mouth and let me see.'

'Really, Mother!' said Krishna as if he couldn't believe the lengths his mother would go to. He tried to struggle free, but Yashoda held on to him even tighter.

'Come on, Krishna. Open your mouth at once and let me see,' demanded Yashoda, pulling him close to her.

Krishna knew that he wasn't getting very far by struggling. If opening his mouth was the only way to make his mother let go of him, he decided that was what he had to do. He opened his mouth as wide as he could, shrugging his shoulders in exasperation. Yashoda peered into Krishna's mouth, a little embarrassed that she should even have to do such a thing. She blinked. Was she dreaming? She could hardly believe what she was seeing. Yashoda rubbed her eyes and looked again. Surely those couldn't be the planets and the stars that she saw in her son's mouth? Could she really see the sun and the moon? Yashoda was speechless. She was so shocked that she loosened her grip on Krishna's arms.

Seeing his chance, Krishna at once clamped his mouth shut and darted out of the room.

That night Yashoda told her husband Nand about what had happened. Nand laughed and began teasing her about working too hard. Yashoda had expected him to make fun of her. It wasn't really surprising; after all, even she was beginning to doubt what she had seen.

'I don't know,' wondered Yashoda as she lay in bed. 'I love him dearly, but that child has always made me doubt myself. It's extraordinary, but for a moment when I looked into his mouth, I really thought I saw the whole universe inside it. And yet when I looked into his eyes again he was just my naughty, thieving little boy.' She smiled. 'Perhaps I am working too hard - or maybe it is the heat.'

During the hot weather it was usual for everyone to have their chores done before the scorching heat of midday, when children and adults alike rested or slept. It was on one such hot afternoon when everyone else was having a nap, that Krishna lay tossing and turning in the heat. He was thinking about all his most favourite things in the world because try as he might, he just could not get to sleep. His mother had already been to him twice, scolding him for singing too loudly to himself and disturbing her sleep. Krishna didn't mind, but Yashoda was usually so understanding that he tried his best to be quiet.

Thinking about his mother and father, he realised that he was very lucky to have such a happy family. Nand and Yashoda were always kind, and Krishna's older brother Balram found time every day to tell him his favourite stories. Krishna closed his eyes and thought about early mornings, when a light mist from the Yamuna river still hung over the village, and the peacocks with their feathers like sapphires and emeralds descended onto the rooftops, calling to each other. He thought about the gentle-eyed cows and their pinky-white calves; about the bright green parrots chattering in the mango trees; and cool, smooth, sweet BUTTER! OH BUTTER!

Any thought of sleep was impossible for Krishna now. Just thinking about butter made him drool and he jumped up from his bed, determined to find some. Krishna knew that there was none left in his own home because he had eaten it all and been severely told off for it. He paced up and down trying to decide on a plan. Someone in the village must have some! Then he remembered something.

'I know Mother was helping her friend to make some butter yesterday,' he thought. 'I wonder if she has any left?' Krishna decided to go and have a look. If anyone was awake in that house he might be able to ask for some butter. Krishna's own home was quiet, and he knew that it was safe for him to go roaming around the neighbourhood. As he had expected, all sensible people were asleep at that time of day. It was so quiet that even the birds and insects seemed lulled into silence. In such hot weather, the people of Gokul did not stir until the shadows began to grow long, and the sun was heavy and orange in the sky.

The houses in Gokul were always open during the daytime and the village children were used to wandering in and out as they pleased. Krishna, who had led many a butter-raiding expedition around the village, knew exactly where his mother's friend kept her butter and went straight to the back of the house. All was quiet apart from a very faint but familiar creaking sound high in the rafters. Krishna peeped around the doorway cautiously and there, as he had expected, was a large and very heavy clay pot hanging from the rafters. It was surely full of butter. The basket which held the pot swung gently in the light breeze and watching it, Krishna could almost taste the cool, creamy butter in his mouth. He looked over his shoulder quickly, but the house was silent and he realised that since there was no-one awake to ask, if he wanted the butter there was no choice but to help himself.

'After all,' he reasoned, 'this butter isn't going to stay fresh forever. It will have to be used up soon so I might as well have some. Anyway, I shall only have a little taste.'

Krishna found a sturdy three-legged stool near the door and carried it as quietly as he could to a spot just underneath the swaying basket. He climbed up onto it quickly. He felt sure that he could easily reach the pot standing on his tip-toes. Krishna stretched as high as he could, straining his legs and his arms and his fingers until they hurt. It was no use. As much as he tried, he could only just reach the bottom of the basket.

'If only my friends were with me,' he thought desperately. 'It would be so easy to reach if I had someone to help me. The only way I'll manage it is by jumping up at it.' With that, he leapt up, his arms flailing, and swiped at the pot.

CRASH! Krishna fell to the floor and the pot tipped over him as it fell too, covering him with creamy butter. Krishna sat where he had fallen with pieces of broken brown pot all around him, happily scraping butter off himself and cramming as much as he could into his mouth. He was enjoying himself so much that he didn't notice the commotion he had caused in the house. People who had been peacefully asleep, dreaming happy dreams, were running about in alarm, grabbing anything they could find to protect themselves. Such banging and crashing was so unusual at that time of day that everyone was sure that it could only be thieves. They ran towards the back of the house, herding together for safety and wielding sticks and staves. But as they reached the room where the noise had come from, they all stopped in confusion. Where they had expected to find two or three fearsome robbers, they found only one little boy and a lot of mess.

By this time the house was full of shouting villagers dashing here and there. Krishna looked up guiltily from his feast as they crowded around him. He searched anxiously through all the well-known faces in the crowd, hoping that his mother might be there to rescue him. Among all those angry faces there was not one which was friendly. For all the women there, seeing Krishna sitting on the floor smeared with butter and drenched in buttermilk, this was the last straw. They were thoroughly fed up with Krishna's pranks. They knew that the time had come at last to put an end to it. Almost every one of them had had her butter stolen at one time or other, but because they all liked Yashoda for her kindness and generosity, nobody had complained to her about her mischievous son. This time, however, they decided that Krishna would have to be punished.

Two women stepped out of the crowd and pulled Krishna roughly to his feet.

'Oh please! Please! I'm so sorry! I really am!' he yelled at the top of his voice. Krishna had never been treated so roughly before and he began crying and pleading.

It was no use. Nobody was listening to him. He was being dragged out of the house and down the dusty street. The few people who hadn't joined the crowd were standing outside their homes, shaking their heads in disbelief as they watched this unusual procession. There were few children about. The children realised that this might very easily have been happening to them, and had wisely stayed out of the way. Poor Krishna! His wrists were held tightly by the women on either side of him, and he was being prodded and pushed by the people behind as he stumbled down the street.

They soon reached Yashoda's house and the women began calling for her to come out. Yashoda was at the far end of the house, busy getting the fire started for the evening meal. She had heard faint noises outside, and thought that it was some children fighting in the street. As the shouting grew louder, Yashoda realised that someone was calling her name. 'I wonder who could want me at this time of day?' she puzzled. Perhaps it was one of her neighbours needing some extra milk. People often borrowed milk from each other. As she hurried out, however, Yashoda saw that it was not just one neighbour but all of them standing at her door. Not only that, but two of her best friends were holding a very dirty and shamefaced Krishna firmly by the arms.

Yashoda realised at once that Krishna had been stealing butter again. She was embarrassed to see how angry all her friends and neighbours were with her son. This was too much even for Yashoda, who loved Krishna more than anyone.

'I'm so sorry,' she said, almost in tears. 'I have told him again and again how wrong it is to steal butter. I really don't know what to do with him anymore.'

'You could start by punishing him,' replied her friend coldly. 'Just telling him is obviously no good. You must make him understand somehow that people don't like thieves. We can't let him carry on like this!'

As much as Yashoda loved her son, she knew that she would have to teach him a lesson. She was angry enough with Krishna, but she became absolutely furious when she noticed a cheeky smile on his face.

'How dare you?' she shouted at Krishna. 'How dare you smile when you know how wrong it is to steal? You have disgraced our family and you should be ashamed of yourself! Come here at once!'

Krishna didn't know what to do. He had never seen his kind and gentle mother so angry before. Whenever he had been caught stealing butter before, he had always managed to escape punishment by making her laugh with a joke or a smile. This time he knew that neither would work. He fell to his knees.

'O my dearest, kindest mother! Please forgive me! I didn't really mean to steal. You know I would have asked if anyone had been awake, but you see....'

Krishna could see that Yashoda wasn't listening. Before he could say any more, she had pulled him to the bullock post which stood outside their house and began tying him up.

'You can stay here until your father comes home,' she said angrily. 'Everyone passing by will see you and they will know that you are a thief and a very naughty boy!'

Yashoda began to wind the rope round and round Krishna's little body but the tighter she wound it, the looser it seemed to get, and as soon as she managed to tie a knot, it came undone.

The villagers who had been watching Krishna's dressing down with some pleasure were suddenly dumbfounded. They stopped shouting encouragement to Yashoda and began to point at Krishna's head. Yashoda was becoming more and more frustrated as she struggled to tie a knot which refused to be tied, and it only dawned upon her gradually that all the people around her were silent. She looked up to see why everyone was so quiet and turned her eyes in the direction they were pointing. What she saw made her gasp in amazement. Around Krishna's head was a glowing halo which shone brightly in the evening shadows.

The villagers of Gokul began to realise that the halo which shone above Krishna's head could mean only one thing. For years they had marvelled at his bravery and strength. Magic had surrounded Krishna since he was a baby, but in many ways he had been such a normal, even wayward child that they had not thought anything of it. At last they realised that they could not ignore the halo. It could only mean that Krishna was especially blessed, and they were honoured to have him in Gokul. From that day on they began to keep aside butter especially for Krishna, and generally treated him with far more respect than a troublesome little boy usually deserves.

Yashoda would have been the first to admit that all the special attention Krishna got from his friends and neighbours might not be good for him. Sometimes Krishna behaved as if he knew and understood everything, and no matter how wonderful he was, surely no child could pretend to be so wise? Krishna seemed to have an answer for everything, and when he was particularly exasperating, Yashoda used to sit him down to talk to him.

'Don't think you're too clever to learn anything new, Krishna,' she said. 'See all the sadhus and munis who come to our door for food. They are wise because they are old and they have travelled all over the land, meeting all kinds of people. When they are not travelling and teaching, they go into the mountains and forests to meditate. You are only a little boy and you still have a lot to learn.'

Krishna bowed his head and pretended to be ashamed. 'Yes, Mother,' he said meekly. ' You are always right.'

One day when Yashoda was preparing the midday meal, she heard a knock at the front door. She went to see who it was. It was a sadhu, a wise man who had no home and no belongings. He wandered from village to village, only eating what people could afford to give him. It was an honour to give a wise man food, and a

18

sadhu was hardly ever turned away empty-handed. People gave what they could, perhaps a chapati or two from one family, or a small handful of rice from another.

Yashoda could see that the sadhu had very little food in his bowl and since she had just cooked some food, she offered him a proper meal. The sadhu accepted and Yashoda hurried off to fetch some water for him to wash his hands and feet before he sat down to eat. Then she found the largest thali she had and heaped food generously onto it before taking it to the sadhu. The old man was sitting patiently on the floor by the front door. Yashoda put the plate down in front of him and left him to eat in peace.

As soon as the sadhu was alone, he closed his eyes and held his hands together in prayer. He never put a morsel of food into his mouth until he had first given thanks to God and offered Him the first taste. The midday air was still, and there wasn't a sound to be heard. The sadhu began to meditate, calling upon God to bless the food he was about to eat. Suddenly he heard a shuffling noise in front of him, and a munching sound as if someone were eating from the plate before him. Who would dare to steal food from a sadhu's plate? The old man opened his eyes and who should he see? Krishna! Yes, it was Krishna helping himself from the sadhu's plate, and he was smiling as if he was proud of what he was doing.

'Aren't you ashamed of stealing from my plate?' demanded the sadhu angrily.

'*Stealing*?' exclaimed Krishna in surprise. 'I'm not stealing. You invited me! I was playing with my friends outside, not even thinking about food, when I heard you calling my name. You asked me to come and bless your meal!'

The sadhu could hardly believe his ears. Was this child playing tricks on him? The only name he had called was God's, and even that was not aloud. The child couldn't possibly have heard him, unless...

'Well,' said Krishna, smiling a little at the look of amazement on the sadhu's face. 'Do you want me to go away?'

'My Lord,' cried the sadhu. 'You have truly blessed me. Please forgive me for doubting you. I don't know how I could have made such a terrible mistake...'

'Oh, come on,' replied Krishna. He was anxious to get his hands on the sweet, round ladoos on the plate. 'Let's finish our meal.'

Who should be laughing and dancing on Kaliya's head and holding up the missing ball, but Krishna!

KRISHNA THE COWHERD

When Krishna was still a young boy, his family along with some others left Gokul and moved to a village called Vrindavan, further along the Yamuna River. They took their cattle with them and life went on much as it had in Gokul. As soon as boys were old enough to be trusted, they were allowed to take their family's cattle down to the river to drink and graze. All boys looked forward to the day when they would be allowed to do this important job. To be cowherds meant that they had really grown up, and being out of the village also gave the boys a chance to make up new and noisier games without interference from their parents.

It was soon Krishna's turn to be out herding cows with Balram and the other older boys. Ever since his mother Yashoda had tried to tie him up for stealing butter, Krishna had promised never to upset her so much again. He did try hard, but he never managed to be so good that he was out of trouble for long. Krishna knew that if he was herding cows by the river, at least his activities would be out of sight of the adults in Vrindavan, and his mother was less likely to hear about them.

The banks of the Yamuna River were a favourite grazing ground. The cows liked the lush, green grass along the river bank, and the trees there provided cool shade in the scorching summer heat. Beyond the grassy flood plain lay thickly wooded forest. Monkeys from the forest often came down to the river to drink, and the young cowherds enjoyed watching the baby monkeys as they chattered and quarrelled among themselves. There was another good reason for watching the monkeys closely: they were always the first to know if there was any danger lurking in the forest.

Under Balram's watchful eye Krishna became a good cowherd. He had loved cows and their dainty little calves for as long as he could remember, and he took the job of looking after them very seriously. Krishna, more than any of the other boys, kept his eyes and ears open for signs of danger, and his friends soon began to depend on him to alert them.

For some time Krishna had noticed that every so often a choking, poisonous vapour rose from the Yamuna River. At these times the monkeys stayed away, and occasionally a calf that ventured too close to the river died mysteriously. The water seemed to bubble and boil, and once when Balram's ball fell into the river, the water sizzled and spat angrily. Sometimes Krishna noticed a long, dark shadow beneath the surface of the water, but the river was deep and fast-flowing, and Krishna was never sure that the shadow was real.

Krishna took his flute with him wherever he went, and when he was worried about anything, the flute was like a friend to him. Whenever his friends grew tired of playing their games, they would settle down around Krishna and listen to his music. It seemed as if the whole world stopped to listen as soon as he played the first clear note. The frisky calves became quiet and lay down beside their mothers. Even the monkeys and crows stopped their squabbling in the trees, and all the birds and animals on the river bank seemed entranced as they drew near to listen to Krishna's music.

One particularly hot morning, a quarrel broke out between two groups of boys playing with a ball. Each group accused the other of cheating, and soon the air was ringing with taunts and insults. One boy was so infuriated by all the shouting and screaming that he threw the ball into the river, hoping that it would mean the end of the fight. It did not. Instead, all the other boys ganged up against him for losing the ball.

Krishna was standing apart from all the fighting, watching the uproar with exasperation. He was fed up with the constant fighting of his friends. If they didn't have an excuse to fight, they soon found one. He too had hoped that losing the ball would be the end of the quarrel. At last, when he could see that the boys were getting too carried away, he moved in to try to break up the fight.

'Oh, stop fighting over a stupid ball,' he cried. 'Whoever cheated, it's all over now. Why can't we just be friends?'

But the boys weren't listening. The fight had stopped being a war of words and was becoming physical. Krishna knew that he had to put a stop to it soon or someone was sure to get hurt.

'If it's the ball you want,' he shouted, 'I shall go and get it from the river.'

His friends heard him this time. All the shouting and pushing and punching stopped immediately. They all turned to look at Krishna. He couldn't possibly mean it. Everyone knew that the river was deep and fast-flowing. Even a good swimmer would be risking his life if he tried to swim in it, and none of them wanted to put Krishna in danger.

The oldest boy ran up to Krishna at once, looking very ashamed of himself. Being the eldest, he should have known better than to let this ridiculous fight over a game go so far.

'No, Krishna,' he said. 'The ball is not important. We don't want anyone to get hurt, least of all you.' He turned to the others and said, 'Come on, I think we've had enough fighting for one day.'

Krishna sat down under a shady tree and took out his flute. He knew that at times like this, his music was the only thing that could quieten the boys. He closed his eyes and began to play. Before long, boys who had thought that they were sworn enemies were sitting down, leaning against each other under the tree. Others were draped along the branches above them. Krishna began to feel peace settle around him and opened his eyes slowly. He loved playing his flute as much as everyone else liked listening to it, and he made up his tunes as he went along. The air was warm and still, and there was scarcely another sound.

Suddenly, Krishna noticed unusual ripples in the river. He continued playing but watched the movement carefully, knowing that it could mean danger. There were plenty of fish in the river, but Krishna knew that whatever was moving around in the water, it was not a fish. He had seen the water move mysteriously like this before. For some time, the villagers in Vrindavan had been talking about a gigantic many-headed cobra which they said lived in the river. They called it Kaliya, and although it hadn't been seen for some time, they said that the. cobra came to the river bank to hunt. If ever a calf disappeared there, the villagers were sure that it had been taken by Kaliya. After all, a calf couldn't disappear into thin air. The villagers were so worried that all the young cowherds had been warned to take special care when they were herding cattle along that stretch of the river.

Krishna was not sure what to do. Should he shout a warning to his friends, disturbing them as well as the animals? Or should he carry on playing his flute and hope that the snake, if that was what it was, would go away without causing trouble? If he called out to the other boys, Krishna knew that his cries might scatter everyone towards the danger rather than away from it. On the other hand, if the snake was determined to take a calf or even a boy, the best thing would be for them all to get away from the river bank as fast as possible. Krishna was still puzzling over what to do. Suddenly he saw that the ripple in the river was slowly moving towards a calf which was dozing just on the edge of the bank. Krishna stopped playing his flute at once.

'Watch out!' he cried. 'It's Kaliya - get out of the way!'

Before Krishna knew what was happening, there were boys and animals running about everywhere in panic, and in all the confusion, nobody was watching the snake.

The cobra began to rise menacingly out of the water. Krishna realised at once why even the adults in his village were so frightened of Kaliya. With the water dripping down his body, the snake was as big and black as a monsoon cloud, and his many heads were fanned open so wide that they shut out the sun. Kaliya's hiss made the sound of a rushing wind, and its eyes were as red as the dying sun.

'I must do something!' thought Krishna desperately. 'This monster will destroy us all unless I stop it!'

Just then Kaliya moved, hissing and spitting towards Krishna as he stood bravely alone on the river bank.

'Alright!' shouted Krishna. 'I'll teach you to come hunting our calves!' and with a shriek of anger, he leapt fearlessly into the Yamuna River.

For a while, all that the other boys could see were Krishna's blue arms and legs thrashing and splashing in the river, and Kaliya's shiney black coils winding around him. Balram and the other cowherds were sure that Krishna would never come out of this fight alive, but they were too frightened themelves to help him. Then, without warning, the water became still once again and all the boys rushed to the edge of the bank to see what had happened. The river was deep, and all they could see was darkness.

Beneath the surface, Krishna and Kaliya were still fighting, but they were sinking deeper and deeper into the water. Finally they reached the river bed. There, among the sand and the rocks was Kaliya's home, and the snake's many wives and children were waiting for their meal. They swarmed around anxiously as they watched Kaliya and Krishna wrestling and tussling together. Kaliya had never had to fight any man or beast for so long before, and although it was so much bigger than Krishna, it began to tire at last. As soon as Krishna felt the snake getting weaker, he saw his chance. He quickly put his arms around Kaliya's massive coils, and began to squeeze. He squeezed so hard that the snake suddenly went limp.

Kaliya's wives and children were horrified when they saw what was happening. They began squirming in despair and pleading with Krishna.

'My Lord, please spare our husband,' they begged Krishna. 'We will do anything if you let him go.'

Krishna felt sorry for Kaliya's wives, and for the little ones. After all, it wasn't so long ago that he himself was only a small child. He had no wish to kill the father of these baby snakes and he knew that Kaliya was too tired to hurt him now.

'I shall let Kaliya live on one condition,' he said. 'You must all promise to move away from this part of the river, and you must never attack people or cattle again. I want you to prove to the people of Vrindavan that you will never harm us again.'

'What shall I do, O powerful one, to show your people that I shall never prey upon them again?' asked Kaliya.

'You may carry me to the surface of the water,' replied Krishna, 'and everyone will be able to see that you have not harmed me, and that they too will be safe.'

Kaliya was so happy that Krishna had not killed him that he agreed to do exactly as Krishna asked. He lay down along the bottom of the river and Krishna clambered onto his head. Slowly, the snake began to swim up towards the top of the water.

By this time, the whole population of Vrindavan had gathered near the river, including Krishna's parents, Nand and Yashoda. Everyone was sad and standing quietly as the best swimmers in the village threw sticks into the water. They needed to know which places were free of poison before they dived for Krishna in the river. Nobody expected to see him alive again. They all knew that Krishna was strong and brave, but the cowherds had seen how enormous and powerful the snake was. Even if Kaliya hadn't squeezed him to death, Krishna was sure to have swallowed some of the poisoned water, which everyone knew was deadly. Those who were going to search for Krishna knew very well that they might die as soon as they touched the water, but they loved Krishna as much as their own children, and they were ready to take that chance.

Yashoda stood apart from the crowd. She could not bring herself to go to the spot where Krishna had jumped in. The thought of her little Krishna lying dead in Kaliya's lair under the water horrified her, and she feared for the lives of the swimmers who were going to search for her son. There seemed to be patches of water which were free of poison, but how could they be sure it was safe?

Suddenly there was a tremendous splashing and the water turned black as Kaliya swam upwards. As the cobra's head rose out of the water, an amazing sight was revealed. Who should be laughing and dancing on Kaliya's head and holding up the missing ball, but Krishna! The crowd backed away in fear, but Kaliya swam carefully up to the river bank and laid Krishna down gently. As he stepped down from Kaliya's head, Krishna looked around him and saw how astonished everyone was.

'I'm not hurt at all! Look!' he cried as he ran in and out of the crowd of villagers. He skipped down to Kaliya again and stroked the snake gently. Then, turning to his family and friends he said, 'Kaliya will never hunt here again. See how gentle he can be.' His promise fulfilled, Kaliya was anxious to get back to the river bed and slowly, with a flick of its forked tongue, it turned and slipped back into the river again.

Krishna's parents as well as all his friends and neighbours were laughing and crying with happiness at seeing Krishna alive and well. Krishna ran to his parents, jumping up to hug them. Yashoda didn't want to let him go again, but when everyone had calmed down enough, she allowed Krishna to sit in the middle of them all and tell his story.

Krishna enjoyed all this attention so much that he rolled and twisted and squirmed on the grass, acting out the fight for everyone's benefit.

'And so,' he panted as he dropped down at last, 'I squeezed and squeezed and squeezed so hard that Kaliya went as limp as a rope! But then I felt so sorry for his family that I decided to let him go, but only if he promised never to bother us again. I don't think he will, do you?'

What could anyone say?

Krishna's eyelids began to droop... and before he knew it, he was fast asleep.

RADHA, KRISHNA AND THE GOPIS

As much as Krishna liked being by the banks of the Yamuna River herding cattle, there were times when he wished that he had an excuse to stay in the village. It wasn't that he didn't like the freedom he had, or the games that he played with the other cowherds: He did. But unlike the other boys, who wouldn't have been seen anywhere near girls, Krishna liked playing with the gopis just as much, if not more. Not only were these milkmaids in charge of making butter, which was temptation enough as far as Krishna was concerned, but it was obvious that they too loved to have him near them.

From the day, as a baby, that Krishna learned to smile, he had charmed all the women and girls of his village. There was always someone to hand when he cried, and if he was hungry they rushed to fetch him food. Whenever he wanted to play, they set aside their work and played with him. And, of course, they always saved him some of the butter they had made for him. In return for all this love, Krishna was always charming and cheerful, and ready with jokes and kisses whenever he found a gopi looking sad.

The conversation among the gopis was always about Krishna and which one amongst them he loved the most. The girls never seemed to talk about anything else. Each gopi was quite sure that Krishna loved her more than anyone and boasted to the others, telling them stories which might or might not have been true.

One gopi, Radha, found the other girls' obsession with Krishna very irritating. Any fool could see that Krishna loved her more than anyone. She pretended not to care, but Radha wished that Krishna would do something to show the other girls once and for all that he loved only her.

'The next time he comes to play with us, I'm not going to follow him like a calf running after its mother,' she promised herself. 'If he really loves me, he will stop chasing the other girls and play only with me.'

Blind Man's Buff was a very popular game with all the children. All they needed for it was a piece of cloth, and they could start and stop playing the game whenever they were called to do a chore. Krishna liked that game too, but for very different reasons. He liked it because it gave him a chance to chase the gopis without worrying their mothers. Krishna always insisted on being the one to wear the blindfold. Anyone serious about the game would have found it easy enough to catch the gopis. The bells on their anklets always betrayed them, but Krishna liked to make a great performance of chasing the gopis. When he did finally catch a girl, he pretended that he couldn't tell who she was without kissing her. The gopis knew about Krishna's trick and had it been any other boy, they would have stopped playing the game long ago. The other boys made fun of Krishna for spending so much time with the girls, but he didn't mind.

There came a time when Krishna's love of playing with the gopis saved their lives. It was a hot day in late summer and the gopis had been up since dawn, milking cows and making yoghurt and butter. Making butter took a long time. It was a hard job and the gopis helped each other as much as possible. It was always a great occasion, and the gopis beat and whisked to the rhythm of their songs. When the butter was finally made and stored away, the gopis decided to go down to the river to bathe, and to wash their clothes which were spattered with buttermilk. It had been hot work and a swim was the best thing to cool them down. They gathered up some clean clothes to change into and set off for the river.

The heat from the sun burned through the cloth which covered the gopis' heads. It even seemed to suck out all the moisture from the grass, which had grown thin and hard and brown. The air was as dry and hot as the inside of an oven, and the ground was baked hard. Mirages of water shimmered in every direction, but the only water for miles around was in the river, and even that was low. The sight of the water brought little relief to the gopis' eyes. It glittered and glared, almost blinding them, and it was only when they reached the dark shade of some trees on the river bank that the gopis began to feel better. They put the bundles they were carrying down in the shade and jumped into the water, grateful for its coolness. Soon they were splashing each other and laughing, chattering like parakeets. Their voices rang out like bells in the countryside, and anyone passing who heard their cries knew at once to keep away.

Anyone that is, except Krishna, to whom the gopis' voices were like a temple bell drawing the faithful to prayer. Krishna was passing by with the other cowherds to grazing grounds further down the river. In some places the grass was still good enough for grazing, and each day the cowherds chose a different spot. They knew that if the cows fed too often from the same place, the land would become over-grazed and bare.

Some boys led the cattle at the front, and others followed behind to round up any strays. Krishna was one of the last in the procession. Chasing after wandering cows was thirsty work, and as soon as Krishna heard the gopis by the river, he started running in their direction. One of the boys called after him.

'Where are you going, Krishna?' he shouted.

'I'm thirsty!' replied Krishna. 'Don't wait for me, I'll catch up with you in a minute.'

Krishna went down to the river taking care to keep out of sight of the gopis, and scooping up some water in his hands, he drank until he was satisfied. He might have turned away and gone back to the other cowherds at once if one of the gopis had not started singing. It was a voice that Krishna would have known anywhere, and it belonged to Radha. To Krishna's ears it sounded as if Radha was singing for him alone, and he stood mesmerised and listened.

Radha's melody floated in the air sweeter than birdsong, and Krishna knew that he couldn't possibly go away without even getting a glimpse of her. He looked around to make sure that none of the other boys had followed him. If anyone caught him near the girls while they were bathing, he knew that they would never let him forget it, and he would certainly be in trouble at home too. The other boys were sensible. They had heard the gopis too, but they knew better than to follow Krishna. As far as they were concerned, if Krishna wanted to get himself into trouble, that was his affair.

Krishna could see that he was safe from prying eyes and he crept up to where the gopis were swimming. He watched them as they put lotus flowers around their necks and in their hair, and he smiled as they admired their reflections in the water. All the girls were very pretty, like flowers themselves, and Krishna began thinking up a plan to make each one of the girls give him a kiss. He saw the bundles of clothes in the shade, and he decided to hide them.

'I'll let them have their clothes back only if they promise to kiss me first,' he said to himself. He gathered up the little bundles and climbed into a tree before the gopis had time to notice that they were gone. Then he sat on a branch and waited.

Krishna did not have long to wait. Their swim had made the gopis hungry and they soon began to talk about going home. Radha half-covered her eyes with her hand, shading them against the glare of the sun, and began looking for her own bundle of clothes. She knew that all the bundles had been piled together in the shade, but where were they now? Radha called out to the other girls.

'Has any of you moved the clothes?' she asked.

The girls all looked at each other in surprise, and then at the spot where their clothes had been. They were mystified. Sometimes one of them did play a trick on the others, but this time they knew that none of them was to blame. What had happened to the clothes?

Krishna could hardly contain himself as he watched the girls' confusion. If only they could see themselves! He tried not to make a noise as he rocked on the branch trying to control his laughter. It was no use. The branch he was hiding in soon began to shake as if there was a troop of monkeys jumping about on it, and Krishna screeched aloud with laughter. The gopis looked up at once. They knew that laugh very well indeed, and now they knew who had stolen their clothes. Sure enough, there was Krishna perched in the tree, as blue as a peacock. Radha glared at him in disgust. This was just typical of Krishna, and he didn't look the slightest bit ashamed. She refused to speak to him but the other girls were already pleading with Krishna.

'Please, Krishna, let us have our clothes back,' they begged.

'Certainly,' said Krishna. 'You can have your clothes back as soon as every one of you gives me a kiss.'

'Oh, Krishna,' they cried. 'Our mothers are waiting for us at home and we're in a hurry.'

'Good!.' replied Krishna. 'The sooner you agree to give me a kiss, the sooner you can all have your clothes back.'

'Have pity on us,' they all implored. 'We are wet and cold now. We'll kiss you after we are dressed.'

'No kiss, no clothes,' laughed Krishna.

'Don't be silly, Krishna, we can't let you see us like this,' they chorused.

'Don't worry, I'll close my eyes. I promise not to look,' he answered.

The girls could see that they weren't getting anywhere by pleading with Krishna, and they crowded together to decide what they should do. Krishna settled down in the tree to wait. He knew that sooner or later the gopis would give him the kisses he wanted. There was no hurry. In fact, he was so warm that he felt like joining them in the river. Even in the leafy shade the air was hot and stifling. The ground below seemed to throb with heat, and Krishna found it difficult to keep his eyes open. Far away he could hear the faint sound of cow-bells, and occasionally, a shout from one of his friends.

He ought really to go back to them after all, but he was so comfortable that even thinking about moving was an effort. Krishna tried to keep himself awake by arranging the bundles here and there on the branches. He gazed at them with half-closed eyes. The bundles hung from the branches like huge, heavy fruit. Huge and heavy...Krishna's eyelids began to droop. They felt heavy... and before he knew it, he was fast asleep.

Minutes later, a passing fire demon came upon this tranquil scene. As everyone knows, demons are the natural enemies of peace and happiness, and the mere sight of Krishna dozing quietly in the tree was enough to annoy the fire demon.

'I shall soon snap this blue boy-wonder out of his sleep,' thought the demon viciously. He began to roll in the parched grass and over the bushes until they started to smoulder and then burst into flames. When they were alight, he jumped over the river onto the other side and started more fires there. The flames leapt from bush to bush, setting everything ablaze. Soon smoke was billowing up through the trees and rising high into the sky.

Krishna woke up coughing. The air was filled with a choking darkness which stung his eyes until tears ran down his cheeks. Krishna couldn't see where the fire had started but the flames were everywhere and the sound of the roaring, crackling fire filled his ears. Krishna was stunned. How could things be so peaceful one minute and fraught with danger the next? Gradually, as his ears began to get used to the noise, Krishna heard the gopis crying for help.

'Get out!' he called back. 'Get out onto the other bank!'

'We can't!' cried Radha over the noise of the inferno. 'The fire has spread to the other side too.'

How could that be? Krishna knew that somehow he had to rescue the girls, but first he had to see how far the fire had spread. He began climbing higher up the tree. The branches became thinner the higher he climbed, and Krishna had to be very careful. One false move and he would fall into the flames below. He could see across the river more clearly now that he was at the top of the tree. Radha was right. Both banks of the river were alight and the fire was spreading quickly in both directions. Krishna began to realise that the safest place for the gopis was in the river itself.

'Stay where you are,' he shouted. 'The fire can't possibly harm you in the water, but make sure you don't get too close to the banks. Even the water is hot there.'

Krishna had to think of himself too. He knew that he couldn't stay in the tree for much longer. The flames were already licking at the tree trunk and it wouldn't be long before the whole tree, large as it was, began to burn too. If the worst came to the worst he could always jump into the river, but the whole countryside was as dry as a tinderbox and if the fire wasn't stopped soon, it would spread to the forest nearby, and that would be a catastrophe.

There was one thing about the fire which bothered Krishna more than anything else. He knew that the heat of the summer sun over dry land could start a fire on one side of the river, but it was strange to see both sides on fire. Water was a natural fire-break and it was too much of a coincidence for two fires to start on opposite sides of the river at the same time. It was so strange that it seemed positively unnatural.

As if the demon had read his mind, a flame suddenly leapt onto the topmost branch out of nowhere. Krishna tried to blow it out at once, but every time he blew one flame out, another flame sprang up in a different place. This was so odd that Krishna knew this could not be an ordinary fire. Only a fire demon could appear and disappear like this. Krishna was trapped. The whole tree would soon be covered in flames, and there was fire below him on the ground too. He drew a deep breath of despair.

The flames around him disappeared as if by magic! Krishna tried it again, and the same thing happened. Now he knew what to do. He began to take huge breaths, swallowing in surprise as he felt something burning pass down his throat. When there wasn't a single flame left on the tree, Krishna shouted to the gopis.

'You're safest in the river,' he yelled. 'Duck under the water quickly and try to stay there as long as you can!'

He had no time to make sure they had obeyed. As soon as he had called out his warning he jumped down into the fire below. Sucking the fire into his body had worked on the tree, and Krishna began to do the same thing on the ground. He opened his mouth and took deeper and deeper breaths. In no time at all, Krishna managed to make a fire-free space around him; and the harder he sucked, the more strength he seemed to have. Soon his breath was as strong as a tornado, sucking away the flames from every bush and blade of grass. The fire demon was no match against Krishna, and before long he was dead.

By the time the smoke had cleared, the gopis were already out of the water and kneeling by Krishna's side. He was lying in a heap of smoking cinders, panting with exhaustion. His lips were scorched, and his throat and lungs were sore. He lay there with his eyes closed, barely moving while the gopis fussed over him, cooling him down with water from the river. Radha knelt by Krishna's head, weeping and stroking his hair. Could anyone live, having fought such a ferocious fire all on his own? Radha felt that she might never be able to tell Krishna how much she loved him. He meant more to her than anything else in the world. Would she ever have the chance to show him that she forgave him, and that she didn't care how many other girls he kissed?

Radha's tears fell softly on Krishna's face. They were warm and somehow comforting to him. He opened his eyes slowly and looked into Radha's face.

'Don't cry, Radha,' he said in a faint voice.

Seeing Krishna trying to smile, Radha sobbed even harder.

'Oh, Krishna, will you ever forgive me for being so angry with you?' she wept. 'I shall never be angry with you again, whatever you do. Your poor lips! Here, let me kiss them better. Don't say anything! If it hadn't been for you, we might all be dead. I know you only stole our clothes to save us from the fire. You always know just what to do...'

Krishna could hardly believe his ears.

'No, you don't understand,' he began, but Radha put her hand over his mouth.

'Don't say anything,' she said. 'I know what you're going to say, and it doesn't matter.'

Krishna gave up. What would Radha say if she ever knew the truth? He closed his eyes in shame. He had never realised how much Radha loved him. All he had wanted was kisses from all her friends, not caring at all that he might be hurting her feelings. And now she thought that he had been trying to save them from the fire. Would Radha ever forgive him if she learnt what he had really done? There and then, Krishna made up his mind never to deceive her again.

The gopis had other ideas. From the day of the fire all each gopi could think about was how wonderful Krishna was. Every girl was certain that Krishna loved her more than anyone and secretly hoped that he might one day marry her. Whenever one of the gopis saw Krishna on his own she followed him, begging him for a word, a smile, a kiss. Krishna wouldn't have minded if it had been Radha following him around, but for some reason she kept well away from him. Life wasn't the same for Krishna anymore. The fun had gone out of chasing and playing with the girls. In fact, he began to feel like a hunter's prey. He couldn't go anywhere without bumping into one of the girls, and they pestered him so much that he began to avoid them as much as possible.

The other cowherds watched Krishna's discomfort with delight. It was about time Krishna got as good as he gave.

'Finding the girls too hard to handle?' they taunted him loudly.

Krishna tried his best to ignore them, but they were supposed to be his friends after all. He was miserable. Radha didn't want anything to do with him and he thought he knew why. He could understand that she didn't like all the other girls chasing after him, but what could he do? Even though he wasn't encouraging them, if something didn't change soon, Radha would probably never speak to him again.

Krishna lay in bed at night, trying to think what to do. There was no point in asking the other boys to help him. They would just laugh. He gazed out of the window at the half-moon which glowed high in the sky. It was autumn and the moon would soon be full. The night of the autumn full-moon was always a special one for the villagers. There was music and dancing...

'Oh no!' thought Krishna as he realised what that meant. "Those girls will be after me all evening, and I know they will make a fool of me. I wish I could split myself up into lots of Krishnas. If each one of the girls could have me to herself, they might all stop bothering me.'

As he lay there thinking about it, Krishna realised what a wonderful idea it was. He knew very well what effect his flute-playing had on the gopis, so it would be easy enough to charm each girl into thinking he was dancing only with her.

'If I can make them think that their dream has come true,' thought Krishna, 'I will be able to spend the whole evening dancing with Radha only.'

His problem settled, Krishna drifted happily off to sleep.

The night of the full moon was magical. The moon hung low on the horizon like a huge copper bowl and a mellow, golden light lay over the countryside. The evening air was cool and fragrant with the scent of flowers. Jasmin, rose and frangipani. In the village, the cattle were safely inside and the babies were fed and already asleep in their beds. The gopis dressed themselves in silk and gold. They put kohl round their eyes and flowers in their hair. The cowherds changed out of their dusty clothes and put on clean, fresh ones. When everyone was ready, the musicians began to play, and Krishna waited with his silver flute.

The moment the music started, all the girls in the village arranged themselves into a huge circle to dance the raas. All of them including Radha had eyes only for Krishna. He stood in the middle of their circle like a blue sapphire in a golden ring. The girls danced as if hypnotised by Krishna's flute music, totally unaware of anything except Krishna and the melody. They spun and twisted, faster and faster, until everything was a blur. Suddenly, could it be true? Each gopi was dancing with Krishna, swaying and swinging in his arms. The only one dancing alone was Radha.

'Oh, Krishna,' thought Radha as she watched the other girls whirling around her. 'Why must you do this to me?'

'Do what, Radha?' she heard.

Radha couldn't believe it at first but Krishna was actually by her side, and whispering in her ear.

'What's the harm in letting them dream?' he said quietly. 'You and I know that we belong only to each other. That is no dream.'

Krishna leapt onto the bull's back and pulled its horns as far back and down as he could.

KRISHNA IN DANGER

As Krishna grew older his fame spread beyond the village of Vrindavan. In the villages and towns all along the Yamuna river, people were talking about the extraordinary blue boy and his amazing exploits. Priests and peddlars who travelled through the kingdoms told and retold the stories of Krishna's brave feats. Adults and children alike marvelled at the tales of Krishna's power.

It wasn't long before these tales reached the ears of Krishna's evil uncle Kans, the King of Mathura. Kans' tyrannical reign had grown harsher as the years passed. The merest sight or sound of an innocent child playing was enough to send him into a rage. Kans could never forget that somewhere beyond the borders of Mathura there lived a boy, his sister's eighth child, who might kill him one day. Kans had murdered every baby boy in Mathura, and each time he heard about an unusual boy in another kingdom, he secretly sent one of his demons to kill the child.

When Krishna was only a baby, Kans had sent a female demon called Putna to Gokul. Putna was ordered to trick her way into Yashoda's home, and to kill the infant Krishna as soon as she had won his trust. Yashoda had been charmed by this woman who seemed so kind and friendly, and she had allowed her to play with Krishna and nurse him. Having won the mother and child's confidence, Putna had tried to poison Krishna with her milk. Krishna had sucked contentedly at her breast but as he sucked, the poison which was meant to kill him began to work on Putna herself. Yashoda had been horrified to discover Krishna playing innocently beside the dead she-demon, and within days, everyone in and around Vrindavan had heard the story.

Kans also heard about Krishna's fight with Kaliya the giant cobra, and he became so fearful that he shut himself away to plot Krishna's death. Kans knew that any child that was capable of defeating such a terrible snake could just as easily destroy a man. Kans could never feel safe while Krishna was alive, and he decided that only the most powerful demons would be able to help him.

One dark night, when the moon was as thin as a sliver of glass and even the stars were hiding, Kans began to summon up his demons. Deep in his palace with only a single candle for light in the dark and dingy room, he sat muttering ·magic spells which had taken him years to master.

'O most powerful Rakshasas who have fed upon the babes I have killed, come to me and help me now!' he called out at last, and soon the room began to grow cold and the candle spluttered and died, leaving Kans shivering in the dark. As he waited, unable to see or hear anything, Kans began to sniff at the familiar smell of sulphur which grew stronger as the demons began to appear.

First came Vatasura, then Bakasura, and finally Bakasura's brother, Aghasura. Each Rakshasa was uglier than the last, with eyes glowing like hot coals, pointed ears, and fangs and nails as sharp as knives. They wore necklaces made of little skulls which clattered and rattled in the gloom, making even Kans' teeth chatter in fright.

'What is your desire, my lord Kans?' boomed Vatasura.

Kans, who was dwarfed in the demon's shadow, found his voice at last.

'There is a boy in Vrindavan whose fame has spread through the kingdoms,' he said. 'People say that he can fight all kinds of monsters. It is said that he is very dark and that he can charm people and animals alike when he plays his flute. I have tried everything to kill him myself, but now I know that he is no ordinary child. I believe that he must be my sister Devaki's boy. It is predicted that her eighth child will slay me, and I think that I have found him at last. You will need to use all your evil powers to kill this child.' Kans told the demons about Krishna's fight with Kaliya, and how he had danced on the cobra's head. 'Will you be able to rid me of this boy?' he asked the demons.

'We have powers which even the mightiest animals do not,' replied Bakasura.

'Only gods can fight demons. Fear not. We will attack him when he least expects it. You will not hear from us until we have done as you ask, but remember, for this you will be in our eternal debt.' said Aghasura, and with that the three demons disappeared in a puff of swirling yellow smoke.

Soon afterwards, strange things began happening to Krishna. One day when he was looking for a lost calf on his own, Krishna was attacked by a giant stork. The huge bird swooped down again and again, screeching and snapping with a beak as large as a canoe. It flapped its wings in swishing strokes until the air whirled around Krishna in a fury, pushing him dangerously close to the edge of the river bank. Just as Krishna was teetering on the edge trying to regain his balance, the stork swooped down so low that Krishna could almost touch its beak. At once Krishna leapt up and grabbed the beak, pulling the bird down with all his might. Soon the stork was flapping and squawking on the ground, trying to get away from Krishna. Krishna was determined not to let the enormous bird escape, and prised its beak so far apart that it snapped with a terrific crack. Suddenly the stork became still and began to change its shape. As it died, the great white bird was transformed into the dark and ugly demon Bakasura, with his pointed ears and razor-sharp teeth and nails. The demon did not move again, and when Krishna was quite sure that he was dead, he picked Bakasura up by the feet and flung him as far as he could into the river.

Not long after, Bakasura's brother Aghasura decided to trap Krishna. He turned himself into an enormous python with a body so long that it could spread itself down the mountainside. There he lay in wait for Krishna with his mouth open wide so that it looked like a cave. Krishna was a curious and adventurous child who often led his friends on exploring expeditions in the hills and valleys. He soon discovered this new cave and called his friends to go inside with him and have a look.

'Look at these strange pink walls!' exclaimed one child.

'Ugh! They're all slimey and wet!' cried another.

Soon the children were stamping and scraping inside the python's mouth, and as they all trooped in, Aghasura began to find it very difficult to breath. He had been hoping to swallow Krishna whole, but he hadn't bargained for this army of children marching into his mouth. Aghasura rapidly began to choke. All his huffing and puffing washed great waves of hot air over the children, and the boys and girls panicked, charging out of the strange cave as fast as they could.

Krishna was the last to come out, but before joining the other children he rolled an enormous boulder into the python's mouth, pushing it in as far as it would go. Krishna and his friends watched from a distance as the python began to melt before their very eyes into an oozing, gooey mess. Soon, all that was left was an enormous pair of jaws around the boulder, and the grotesque body of Aghasura, thrashing and rolling as he died.

Krishna became quite a hero after all this and before long, the young cowherds of Vrindavan didn't feel at all safe unless Krishna was with them. Krishna himself naturally enjoyed all this admiration, and he also began to feel that it was his duty to help and protect his friends. He liked nothing better than to sit on the river bank playing his flute, while the cattle grazed quietly and the boys played their games.

One afternoon, Krishna had just finished playing a tune when he noticed that instead of being lazy and sleepy as they usually were at this time of the day, the cows were restless and crowding together nervously. Their bells jangled loudly in the quiet countryside and woke the other boys who had been napping in the shade. Krishna stood up quickly to investigate. He squinted in the glaring sunlight, trying to see what was going on.

'I have never seen the cows so disturbed,' thought Krishna.

Suddenly he noticed that there was a bull among the cows and calves. He knew that bulls were not usually allowed to graze with the cows because they were more or less wild and very bad-tempered. This was certainly not their own village bull. Could it be a stray? Some bulls were so unpredictable that even the best handlers couldn't control them, and they were left to roam as they pleased.

Cattle were so important to farming people that it was forbidden to kill them, even if they were sometimes dangerous.

This bull was white, nearly twice as big as the cows and its horns were curved and as long as swords. It began to snort and scrape at the ground with its hooves. The cows started to low in alarm and rolled their eyes in fear as the bull suddenly turned towards Krishna, bent down its head, and charged. There was mud and grass flying everywhere as the bull thundered towards Krishna, who instead of running for cover, stood his ground. The other boys had already fled and were clambering up every available tree.

The bull's horns were so sharp that they could shred man and beast to ribbons, and Krishna knew that all their lives were in danger. At the very least, if the bull wasn't stopped at once the cows and their calves would be scattered all over the countryside, and it would be late into the evening before the cowherds got the herds back together again. There was only one thing to do. Krishna had to fight the bull, subdue it and kill it if necessary.

The bull's horns were as sharp as skewers and Krishna had to make sure that he kept out of their way. As soon as the brute was close enough, he leapt onto its back and pulled its horns as far back and down as he could. The animal was stampeding blindly with its muzzle in the air. It bellowed angrily, straining to push its head down again so that it could see where it was going. Krishna, of course realised that with its head in the air, he could steer the creature wherever he wanted.

He saw a mighty old banyan tree just to the right of him, and pulling the bull's head sharply to the right, he jumped onto the ground out of harm's way. Snorting and bucking with its head still high in the air, the bull crashed headlong into the old tree, shaking it to its very roots. There were clouds of red dust everywhere and at first it was difficult to see exactly what had happened. Krishna lay where he had landed until the commotion had died down; then, he picked himself up from the dust and limped towards the battered banyan tree, calling the other boys to follow him.

'Come on!' he cried, 'That bull had such a bang on its head, it must surely be dead!'

The other cowherds weren't quite so sure, but they began to climb down from their perches, wiping the dust and grit from their eyes and mouths. They didn't feel at all brave but they crowded behind Krishna as they approached the bull. As they drew near to the huge banyan tree, they saw that the mighty white body of the bull was changing colour and shape. The massive bull had begun to wither away and in its place at the foot of the tree was a hideous, dark creature with pointed ears, and teeth and nails sharper than scythes. It was Vatasura.

As soon as the boys were certain that there was no life left in the demon, they tied him up with a rope and rolled him into the river. Soon, the demon Vatasura was sinking slowly into the Yamuna River, and all that remained to show what had happened was a large dent on the trunk of the banyan tree.

'When have you ever seen a mountain playing a flute?'

THE LIFTING OF MT GOVARDHAN

The health, wealth and happiness of a farming village like Vrindavan depended on rain. The difference between a good harvest and a bad one was vital to many families, and each year the people waited for the rains to start with longing, and with dread: Too much rain and the land would be flooded and the crops washed away; Too little, and there would be no crops worth harvesting at all. It was not unknown for whole villages to be ruined by too much or too little rain, and a farmer could never be sure that there would be just enough to raise good crops and healthy cows. As far as the farming people were concerned, whatever happened to them depended on the will of the gods.

It was not surprising, with their lives so full of uncertainties, that the people of Vrindavan depended upon the gods and tried to keep them happy. If they were poor they prayed to Lakshmi, the goddess of wealth. For warmth and sunshine, they prayed to Surya the Sun god, and for rain they prayed to Indra, the god of the heavens, rain and clouds. Most of the time, people got what they asked for from the gods, and for them it was proof that their prayers and sacrifices worked. At other times it seemed as if the gods punished people too. Any drought, storm or fire was a sign that a god was displeased.

One year the rains failed. The sky stayed clear and blue longer than it should have, and there wasn't a trace of a rain cloud. The air was still and dry, and the leaves and grass withered in the sun. The earth grew hard and difficult to till. The streams dried up and even the big rivers ran low. There was not a hint of moisture in the air, and as the days and weeks went by, the cattle became thin and lost their milk. The village streets in Vrindavan grew quiet. There were no cries from the children and the women stopped singing. The men sat

49

idle and watched the skies, waiting for the rain. The whole village was lifeless, silent and waiting. There were no fields to plough, no cows to milk, no water to draw.

It became clear to the villagers that their daily prayers at the temple were being ignored. A few more days of this drought and the little babies might begin to die. Why was Indra so angry with them? At last the villagers decided to speak to the priest.

'It is obvious,' said the priest gravely, 'that more than prayers are needed to pacify Indra. You have suffered much, and if Indra has not taken pity on you by now, he must surely be very angry with you. Only a special ceremony dedicated to Indra, with gifts and sacrifices will touch his heart now.'

Gifts... Sacrifices... How would they manage? Only the best food and drink could be presented to the gods, and the villagers had barely enough to feed themselves. Nand, Krishna's father, began to speak to them all.

'Each one of us must give something, however little, and it should be the best that we have,' he said to the people of Vrindavan. 'Go into your homes, your gardens and your fields, and gather whatever you can find. I have a cow who has just had a calf. The calf is dead and the cow is thin. She has very little milk, but what she has I will gladly give up to Indra.'

Impressed by Nand's generosity, the other villagers began wondering what they might give. The women went into their kitchens and scraped together what they could, a scoop of rice, a handful of wheat, or a bowl of milk. The children wandered through the gardens looking for fruit and flowers and the sacred herb, basil. The older boys and girls roamed the forest outside Vrindavan searching for wild berries and flowers, and the men went into their fields to dig up whatever crops had survived.

Soon, all the people of Vrindavan had collected their gifts together. The Brahmin priests were there with the ghee, incense and sandalwood they needed for the ceremony. All the villagers and even the children helped to carry their gifts to a shrine they had built for Indra in the forest. When they had finished arranging all the food and flowers, the priests lit the holy fire and began chanting their prayers.

The children stared wide-eyed at all the food, and their mothers watched their hungry faces with tears in their eyes.

'Please, Indra,' they prayed quietly as they patted their children's heads. 'Take pity on us and send us rain.'

Krishna looked on as the priests offered the food to the rain god. The ceremony seemed like nothing more than a waste of good food to him.

'Look at that!' he said to his father in disgust. 'That food and milk would be better in the bellies of hungry babies.'

'Hush!' said his father fiercely, afraid that Indra might hear. 'For once, Krishna, don't cause trouble. This is too important to all of us.'

'That's ridiculous!' retorted Krishna. 'What good can it do to give away the only food we have, when we are all starving? I can't think of anything more silly than offering food to a stone statue, even if it is supposed to be Indra.' Krishna was quite indignant, and the more his father tried to keep him quiet, the louder his voice grew.

The other people began to shuffle their feet in apprehension, and the priests glared angrily at Krishna. He didn't care.

'But from what I can see,' he continued loudly, 'Indra sends us rain when he feels like it, and it doesn't matter whether we pray to him or not. And when he does send rain, he doesn't seem to care where it falls. It falls on the oceans where it isn't needed at all just as much as here on the land, where we need it desperately. In fact, I don't think Indra controls the clouds and the rain at all.'

When they heard this, the people began shouting at Krishna.

'How dare you insult Lord Indra?' they cried.

'I don't understand you at all,' Krishna yelled back. 'You might as well worship that mountain over there, or Vrindavan forest. We get as much from the mountain and the forest as we seem to from Indra, however much we pray and offer sacrifices. I think we should stop praying to Indra and dedicate this ceremony to Mt Govardhan instead.'

If Krishna had known what was to come, he might never have interfered with the prayers, or perhaps he knew and he wasn't afraid. From the moment his name had been called in prayer by the priests, Indra had opened his eyes. He saw the gifts of food and flowers and the sacred basil, tulsi, and he was pleased. He listened to the villagers' prayers and hymns, and he was contented.

'I will gather my clouds around me, and soon the people of Vrindavan will have their rain,' thought Indra as he gazed down fondly at the villagers' devotion. But when Krishna began ridiculing the villagers and insulting him, Indra's heart turned black in anger. His rage thundered and rumbled in the sky, and his clouds became dark and swollen with fury. 'Is it rain they want?' roared Indra. 'Then they shall have it!'

For countless days and nights, rain poured from the heavens. Thunder rolled in the sky and great shafts of lightning pierced the darkness. The sun died, and hailstones the size of pigeon eggs fell to the earth. A chill, howling wind blew across the land, uprooting trees and hurling them to the ground. Water ran off the hills and mountains in gushing waterfalls, and the rivers burst their banks, spreading water far into the countryside. The very earth seemed to break under the force of the storm, and huge rifts and gullies appeared across the land.

The wild animals from the river and the forest scurried instinctively towards the higher ground, trying to escape the flood waters. Even the creatures which normally lived in the water sensed the danger and fled. At first, the village folk tried to shelter in their homes, but the wind and the rain had weakened their houses and brought them crashing down. After that they stayed under the ruins of their homes for a few more days, too frightened to leave, but there was no warmth and no comfort for them. The air was cold and damp and heavy, and it ate into their bones. Their clothes were clammy and clung to their skin. All around them was a vast, muddy lake, and they watched helplessly as their shattered belongings floated away before their eyes. All the food was wet and rotting, and there was no clean water to drink. Then, inevitably, the little children became feverish and ill. Now the villagers had no choice but to leave.

In the shifting, flowing landscape only one thing remained reassuringly solid: The villagers knew that the only safety they would find was on the higher ground around Mt Govardhan. In the distance the land sloped gradually up from the river valley, and there, rising above the forest and the village of Vrindavan, stood the mountain. If they could manage to reach the foothills of the mountain, they would be safe from the the flood.

Along with all the other creatures in the land, the villagers began to make their way towards the mountain. Those with young babies bundled their infants into baskets which could float. Others carried their children on their backs. The old and weak were put on makeshift rafts made from beds and other furniture tied together with rope. They set off, swimming, desperately clinging to the rafts or clutching at broken branches as they floated by. There was nothing more left for them to lose, only their lives, and what would even they be worth when the flood finally subsided?

Not everyone reached the high ground safely. Those that did were themselves more dead than alive, and hardly understood the loss of their loved ones. They stumbled around in the darkness, trying to find some relief from the rain which had pelted them for days. Would this nightmare ever end? If anything, here on the hillside they were more exposed than ever before. There was nothing between them and the arrows of lightning which hunted them. Their cries drowned in the deafening noise of the thunder, and the people scrambled about like ants, trying to find cracks and caves and crevices to hide in.

Krishna stood apart, alone and silent. No-one else would say it, but he knew who was to blame for this terrible calamity. He was frozen with guilt, unable to move, unable to give help or comfort to the others. Krishna didn't look for shelter. If anyone deserved to perish in the storm, it was he. Nothing could justify the suffering he had caused his people. It was he who had mocked their beliefs and their prayers. It was he who had aroused Indra's anger. When his people had been so desperate for rain, should he not have respected their prayers?

Yet, however badly Krishna felt about what had happened to his people, in his heart he knew that he should not take all the blame for their suffering. They did not deserve to lose everything they had lived and worked for. If Indra had heard Krishna's scornful words and felt insulted by them, surely he should only have punished Krishna? What right had Indra to play with the lives of innocent mortals? These people had always tried to live without harming anyone. They had tilled their land and tended their cattle. They had married and had children and looked after their old folk. They had worked hard, and in everything they did, they had thanked the gods for their happiness. They had prayed for rain, and when their children and cattle had begun to starve, what did Indra do? He forgot their prayers and sacrifices. He forgot their love and devotion. He took offence at the words of a young cowherd, and instead of helping the villagers, he had cursed them.

Krishna was so wrapped up in these thoughts that he hardly noticed the storm which still raged around him. He was angry at the unfairness of it all, but he was so overcome with guilt and despair too, that he couldn't understand his own suffering. He could barely feel the hunger gnawing and gnashing at his insides. His body shivered from the cold, but he hardly noticed it. He was soaking wet. The rain poured over his head and into his eyes, dripping from the end of his nose, but he did not feel it. All he could feel was that he was small, and the wind and the rain, the thunder and the lightning were too big, too fierce for him to resist. How could anyone fight these ferocious forces of nature, least of all a young boy like him?

Krishna felt weak. He closed his eyes. He didn't want to see what was happening to his people. He didn't want to listen to their desperate cries. The wailing echoed in his head. His head began to buzz and he shook it, trying to brush the noise away. Could he be imagining it? Krishna had the strangest feeling of rising up, high in the sky. He stretched and shook his head again. Was it his voice that was calling to the people of Vrindavan? Suddenly Krishna felt as large as the earth and the heavens, stronger than the wind, taller than the clouds. Could it really be his voice that rang out across the skies, louder than thunder?

'Come, my people!' he heard. 'I will give you shelter.'

The villagers heard the voice too, but they couldn't believe it. They were tired and hungry and frightened. It was easy to imagine things. After all they had been through, it seemed too late for anyone to help them. The old and the young clung to each other, frightened that it was a trick. What if Indra was still not satisfied with the damage he had caused? What if he wanted to make sure that none of them lived at all? Everyone was filled with dread.

Then slowly from high up in the sky, the most beautiful flute music drifted down towards them. It was as lovely as Krishna's own music, and the people wondered if they had all died after all. They looked up and began to call out to one another. Suddenly their voices sounded loud. They echoed in the air. The villagers could hardly believe it. All around them the noises of the storm had died down. The wind had stopped tearing at their clothes. There was no more rain running down their faces, and the thunder sounded too far away to matter.

'Look!' cried a little girl. 'It's Krishna!'

The old people shook their heads in pity.

'The child is dreaming, poor thing,' they thought.

'It is Krishna, it is!' began the child again.

Everyone looked up to where the girl was pointing, shielding their eyes against the strange light which filled the sky.

'There!' said a man. 'Can you see his head? And look, I can see his shoulders.'

'Yes,' cried another. 'There are his feet, where the mountain used to be.'

'Silly men,' muttered an old woman scornfully. 'You're as bad as the child. That's the mountain you're looking at!'

'Oh really?' replied the first man. 'When have you ever seen a mountain playing a flute?'

'Well, if that's Krishna, where is the mountain?' demanded the old woman. She shook her head as if she thought the man was stupid.

But where *was* the mountain? The people stared at the enormous apparition which towered above them. Incredible as it seemed, what the girl said was true. It did have the appearance of Krishna. The form had a head and arms and legs, all a deep mauve colour in the darkness. One of its arms was raised above its head. Their eyes followed it up and stared unbelievingly at what they saw. It couldn't possibly be true, but the figure seemed to be holding something up on its little finger. Whatever it was, the object cast an enormous triangular shadow upon the ground.

It seemed, then, as if the sky itself spoke to the villagers.

'Stay under the mountain,' they heard it say. 'You will be safe from the storm under the mountain.'

The people looked around them and saw that what the voice had said was true. They began to understand why the wind had died down. They felt no more cold darts of rain upon them, and they saw that the mountain was indeed covering and protecting them. The storm still raged above the mountain and around Krishna's head, but under the mountain, all was calm.

Krishna's mother Yashoda lay on the ground not understanding what was happening. Surely it couldn't be her own Krishna holding up the mountain as if it were no more than a mushroom? All the others were looking lost and confused too. Their heads were drooping and their bodies ached. In the sudden stillness they began to feel all the tiredness which they had tried to ignore while they were fleeing from the storm. One by one, they began to drop to the ground, their eyes heavy with sleep and relief.

For seven days and nights the people and animals of Vrindavan slept, untouched by Indra's storms. As he watched them sleeping, Indra realised that his energies were no match against the power which had protected these mortals. It was a power that was greater than all the forces of his rain and thunder put together. Indra bowed his head to the shape which loomed up into the sky above him, and he spoke,

'My Lord, you have shown me that all my strength is nothing before you. Your will be done. I will cast away my anger, for I can see that I have wronged your people. May they prosper and be at peace.' With that, Indra dismissed all the dark clouds. He harnessed the thunder and the lightning, and soon the skies were clear and calm.

When the villagers woke up they felt the warmth of the sun upon their faces and on their backs. They looked around them and saw that the waters of the flood had receded and new, green grass was beginning to sprout on the land. The cows that had survived the great flood were pulling contentedly at the sweet grass, and in the distance, the forest echoed with the sound of deer barking. Flowers bloomed on the mountainside and far away, peacocks were calling to their hens.

The villagers heard birdsong, and music from Krishna's flute. The melody was familiar and comforting, and all the people and animals began to gather around Krishna. He leant against the warm, white flanks of a cow, smiling and running his fingers lightly over his flute. A single peacock feather fluttered in his hair, and as they watched Krishna, the villagers began to wonder if the terrible storm had ever happened. Had it all been just a nightmare after all?

He put his arms around the great bird's neck and buried his face in the warm softness of its feathers.

KRISHNA AND GARUDA

After the great flood, the people of Vrindavan tried to pull their lives into some sort of order once again. It was not easy. Almost everything they had had was destroyed. Even before the flood, they had lost their crops and many of their cattle because of the drought. After that, the rain had rotted much of their seed, and now most of their fields were under layers of mud. All that was left of the village and their homes were ruins, but the villagers put aside their sadness and set to work. They knew that only hard work would give them food to eat and homes to live in, so they all helped each other.

The men and women rebuilt their houses as best as they could. When that was done and they all had roofs over their heads, the women took off their gold jewellery and gave it to their husbands. It was all they had to barter for food and seed and tools. They wanted to plough their land and plant new crops as soon as they could. The only good thing that came out of the flood was that the soil was now moist. It was soft and easy to plough, which was just as well, since most of the families had no bullocks to draw their ploughs for them. Soon the seed was sown and in the steady warmth of the sun, the villagers watched their crops as they sprouted and grew, inch by inch each day. If all went well, they would soon have a ripening crop and food would be plentiful once again. They would be able to buy cattle and begin to live their lives normally once more.

The villagers spent all day in the fields, hoeing and weeding, taking care that nothing should destroy their crops once again. The little children chased away birds which pecked at the seedlings. They ran between the furrows, shouting and waving their arms about. The young girls took care of the babies as their mothers worked in the fields, and the boys helped their fathers, pulling the ploughs in teams

59

like bullocks. As each day passed, the villagers began to see the results of their work and soon their fields were green again.

Every year the subjects in Kans' kingdom paid homage to their King. The people of Mathura and the villages around the city always managed to find the cattle and grain which Kans demanded. It was more than their lives were worth to risk arousing Kans' anger. They had seen what could happen to people who didn't pay their taxes. But in the year of the great drought and the flood which followed it, so many of Kans' people were ruined that village after village sent their headmen to plead with the King. Kans cursed them and threatened them with terrible things. Even the sight of the headmen grovelling pitifully at his feet did not touch his heart. Kans' advisers tried to reason with him, but he glared at them until they all fell silent. 'My grain stores are empty,' he told them, 'and I want more cattle. I don't care how you do it, but you must make the people give me what I need. I won't have them thinking that they can get away without paying their taxes.' Seeing his advisers' glum faces, he added shrewdly, 'Don't forget, you too will have a share of all the taxes these peasants pay.'

This persuaded his advisers, just as Kans knew it would. In no time all they were busy muttering together. Soon the chief adviser came up with a plan.

'Your Highness,' he said, smiling slyly. 'Why don't we take what we want from the villages outside our borders? Their rajahs are too frightened of you ever to declare war on you. Once those villages have paid their dues to you they will be as good as yours.

Nothing could have suited Kans better. It was a perfect plan. Not only would he have all the taxes he wanted, but his kingdom would be bigger in the end. Kans summoned his soldiers and told them the plan.

'Take the grain and cattle by force if necessary,' he told them, 'and remember, there will be a reward in it for you too.'

The soldiers went out into the countryside bordering the Kingdom of Mathura, and began to raid the villages. They rode from village to village, plundering as they went. The stories of what Kans' soldiers were up to spread throughout the land and reached Vrindavan before long.

The people of Vrindavan didn't know whether to believe what they heard at first, until one day the soldiers rode into their own village. They cantered into Vrindavan, raising clouds of dust in the streets, and called out the villagers who were hiding in their homes.

'Come out, you miserable wretches,' shouted Kans' soldiers. 'Come out and bring your cattle with you.'

When no-one appeared, the soldiers leapt off their horses and began ramming open the doors. All this was too much for Krishna's father. Nand ran out into the street trying to stop them.

'Who gives you the right to come into our village like this?' he demanded.

One of the soldiers laughed at Nand.

'I'll tell you who gives us the right,' he said. 'The Maharajah of Mathura gives us the right. Now stop arguing with me or I shall take you to Mathura too, along with your cows and your crops.'

'Please leave us something to eat,' begged Nand. 'We need our cattle, and we shall starve if you take all our food.'

'You may keep one cow for each family,' said the soldier, 'but I have seen that your fields are green with new crops, and you must give us all you have.'

Nand tried again.

'Have pity on us,' he pleaded. 'We have young children and old people to feed. You must have your own children too, and parents. Surely you understand...'

The soldier drew out his sword.

'If you don't give us what we want,' he said angrily, 'you won't need to worry about your children or your old folk. We'll make sure there aren't any left.'

These chilling words shocked Nand. Now he knew that there was nothing else but to do as the soldiers commanded. He called Krishna and Balram.

'Fetch the sack of rice we have in the store,' he told them,' and when you have done that, bring out all our cows except one.'

The other villagers followed Nand's example. One by one, the families began to bring whatever they had managed to save out into the street. Before long, most of the village cows were gathered in the street and there was a small pile of rice-filled sacks.

61

'Now,' ordered the soldier. 'I want a cart and a couple of bullocks to pull it. One of you load up the cart as soon as it's ready.'

'I'll do that, father,' volunteered Balram.

'And I'll herd the cows, if you like,' offered Krishna, much to his father's surprise. It was unusual for Krishna to be so helpful, especially when it was a job none of the other villagers would have wanted to do. Krishna was hardly submissive at the best of times. What could he be up to?

Nand wondered if it was wise to let his sons go to Mathura. What if Krishna did something silly and got them all into even more trouble? Krishna saw the look on his father's face.

'Please let us go, father,' he said. 'We want to make sure that everything reaches Mathura safely, don't we, Balram?' He stared meaningfully at his brother.

Balram was puzzled but he replied quickly.

'Of course we do. We want to be sure that the cattle are fit and healthy when they arrive in Mathura, or the Maharajah might punish us.'

Nand shrugged. He knew that there was no point in arguing if the boys had made up their minds. They would go whether he wanted them to or not.

'Alright,' he said, 'but make sure that you come home as quickly as you can. And take care...'

Balram was already harnessing the bullocks to the cart, and when that was done he started loading up the sacks of rice. Krishna tucked his flute out of the way and coaxed the cows together, making gentle clucking noises. The cows nudged closer to each other, obeying the familiar sound of Krishna's voice. Soon the soldiers and the two boys were ready to leave. The soldiers divided up into two groups, so that the two boys with the cart and the cattle were in the middle. The soldiers crowded around them so tightly that neither boy could be seen as the cavalcade left the village.

The journey to Mathura was a quick one on horseback but the cattle slowed them down. The sun was already beginning to sink into the horizon, and Krishna knew that they wouldn't reach Mathura by nightfall. They would probably have to rest somewhere until morning.

'I hope we're going to camp near water,' he said to a soldier at the front.

'We'll be coming up to the river again soon,' replied the man. 'We can camp there for the night.'

It wasn't long before Krishna caught sight of water glittering golden in the evening sun. The day had begun to lose its heat at last, but everyone was looking forward to a drink of fresh, cool water. They pulled up under some trees and let the animals drink. Some of the soldiers began to chop down some branches from the trees.

'What do you think they're up to?' whispered Balram.

'I should think they're making a stockade for the cattle,' replied Krishna quietly. 'Listen,' he said, 'I think we should make a run for it as soon as they are all asleep. I was hoping that we might be able to trick them and get away with the cattle during the journey, but they've been keeping a very close eye on us and I'm quite sure we won't manage it in daylight. I don't think we'll be able to save the cattle, but we can at least try to escape ourselves.'

'Alright,' agreed Balram. 'When should we do it?'

'I don't know yet,' said Krishna. 'Just watch me carefully. We'll have to take our chance when we can.'

It was quite dark by the time all the animals were taken care of. The horses were tethered loosely to the trees, but the soldiers made sure that every one of the cows as well as the two bullocks were safely inside the stockade. Krishna and Balram spoke together as little as possible in case the soldiers became suspicious, but Balram watched every move his brother made. He was ready to go as soon as Krishna gave him the signal. A soldier laughed out loud at something Krishna said, and then Balram heard,

'I'm really looking forward to seeing Mathura. Vrindavan is just a poor, dusty village, and they tell me that Mathura is all gold and marble. I'm so excited that I don't think I'll be able to sleep, but I'd better try. I want to be wide awake when I catch my first sight of your wonderful city.'

Krishna lay awake for a long time after the last soldier had settled down to sleep. He watched the sky as the night deepened and slowly the stars appeared like heavy, silver pendants in the darkness. Krishna's ears picked up the slightest sound. Somewhere in the forest he heard a monkey screeching. Across the river a lonely jackal barked, and a hunting owl flapped by above him. After a while even the animals were quiet, and all Krishna could hear was the sound of flowing water. He sat up cautiously and glanced down at Balram, who was lying beside him. Balram's eyes were open, and as soon as he saw Krishna move, he sat up too. They both looked around to make sure that the soldiers were safely asleep. It was time to go. Soon they would be gone like spirits in the night.

But it was not to be. Krishna should have known that at least one soldier would stay awake on watch. Just when they thought that they were safe, the boys heard a shout. They both froze.

'Don't move!' hissed Krishna. 'They'll never find us in the dark.'

He was wrong. The soldiers were trained to track and fight in the dark, and the two boys were soon captured.

They spent the rest of the night guarded and tied to a tree. In the morning, the captain of the soldiers swaggered up to them.

'I think we'll be able to manage without you from now on, boys,' he said casually. 'You realise, don't you, that your stupid trick is going to cost you your lives? If you have a last wish, speak up now.'

Krishna thought for a moment.

'Will you let me play my flute for a while?' he asked.

'That sounds harmless enough,' replied the captain. "I'll untie you for a while, but don't think you'll be able to get away this time. I'll be watching you.'

Glad to be untied at last, Krishna took up his flute and began to play. The clear notes pierced the misty morning air and filled it with a haunting melody. The soldiers stopped in their tracks and stood perfectly still, spellbound by the music, but in the stockade the cattle began to stir. Krishna carried on playing and soon the cattle were pushing so hard against the stockade fence that it came crashing down. The soldiers didn't even move. They didn't seem to know what was happening. Their eyes were open but they might as well have been asleep.

Krishna and Balram were well away before the soldiers came to their senses and realised what had happened. Nobody volunteered to chase after the two boys. They knew now that the dark boy was a great magician, and the soldiers were more frightened of what he might do to them than they were of their own King. They returned to Mathura with only a few sacks of rice, and stood before Kans in disgrace as their captain tried to explain what had happened. Kans didn't even wait for the captain to finish his story.

'Get out of my sight!' he growled contemptuously. 'Sentries, take this rabble away and make sure that I don't ever see their faces again.'

Kans was furious. Krishna had made a fool of him once too often, but he would soon finish the boy. He summoned the most powerful magician in the land and ordered him to make up a powerful, poisonous potion.

'I can't promise that this poison will kill Krishna,' said the old magician, 'but when he has drunk it, he will be as good as dead.'

Before the next morning dawned, Kans' most trusted servant was on his way to Vrindavan with the flask of poison. The servant walked briskly all day and reached the village just when people were preparing their evening meal. Somehow he had to make sure that Krishna took all the poison. The magician had told him that it had no taste or smell, so if he could sneak it into the boy's food, his job would be done.

The servant hid until he saw Krishna coming home for the day from herding cattle. Krishna had no idea that he was being followed. He was hungry, and the only thing on his mind at that moment was food.

'I'm home!' he called to his mother as he came into the house.

'Your meal is ready,' replied Yashoda. 'I'll set it out for you while you go and wash.'

Krishna splashed water over himself hurriedly and was soon sitting down in front of a plate full of food. There was rice and vegetables and yoghurt, and a large bowl of buttermilk. The buttermilk was just what he needed to quench his thirst. Krishna picked up the bowl and began to drink. He slurped the last drop and was about to ask for some more when everything began to swim before his eyes. He sat there dazed. His hands lay limp in his lap and his eyes stared blankly ahead. Suddenly Krishna felt a hand on his shoulder. He looked up and a kind face smiled at him.

'Come, my child,' said the face. 'We have far to go.'

A man pulled Krishna up and led him away. Krishna followed the man. For how many days he didn't know. He didn't even notice that after a while, the lush greenness of the countryside he knew so well was gone. The trees and bushes grew further apart, and the ground they were walking on became reddish and warm to the touch. Then, there were no more trees or bushes. No shade. No water. Krishna's feet were blistered and bleeding, his face raw and burnt. The harsh sunlight stung his eyes, but still he followed the man, stumbling, falling and picking himself up again. Krishna's ears were deaf to the silence around him, and his eyes saw nothing but the feet in front of him. Hours of light followed hours of darkness, and then... then, there was nothing but darkness.

Krishna lay in the desert hardly alive, and yet not dead. Like a stone he lay unmoving as the desert creatures, ants and lizards, crawled over him, savouring the dried, salty sweat on his body. His hair became matted with wind-blown sand and sun-dried dew, and his eyes and mouth were clogged with dust. With only the sky above him and the earth below, Krishna was scarcely a part of this world or the next. If Yama Rajah, the King of the Dead had come calling his name, Krishna would not have known it. Who was Krishna? Where was he? He didn't know. He was nothing. A desert rock, a puff of wind.

There was a flutter in the stillness. Was there a sound stroking his ears? Krishna stirred. It was too loud. No, it couldn't be a noise. There was nothing here, just comforting emptiness. A wave of warm air wafted over Krishna's body. He cringed. There was that noise again, a heavy flapping sound. Gentle fingers of light began to prise open his eyes. He screwed them shut. The light and the sound probed his body, nudging him to life. Krishna tried to turn away but the darkness was slowly going and through his closed eyelids he began to feel the red warmth of light around him. He opened one eye a tiny crack and closed it again at once. The brightness was blinding.

The noise began again, more persistent this time. Krishna tried to shut it out but every movement he made wracked his body with pain. His head rang with the noise. He kept his eyes closed to keep out the light, but suddenly the redness went away and instead a soothing, grey coolness covered him. Krishna's eyes felt shaded from the glare and he opened them gingerly. A pair of ringed, amber eyes stared down at him.

'Are you awake, My Lord,' said a voice gently.

Krishna's eyes shifted, searching for the mouth that spoke the kind words. But it wasn't a mouth. It was a beak: Sharp and curved and lethal like an eagle's. Krishna gazed in wonder at the shape before him. It was a bird, but larger than any bird he had ever seen, with golden feathers which gleamed in the sun. Krishna squinted up at it.

'Who are you?' he mumbled.

The bird cocked its head to one side and closed one brilliant eye.

'I am Garuda, King of the Birds and surveyor of the skies,' it replied. 'I have come to help you. Climb onto my back and I will find you food and water.'

Food. Water. It seemed so long since Krishna had even thought about eating and drinking. Suddenly, unbearably, his throat gagged with dryness and his empty stomach churned in pain. Seeing Krishna weakening again, Garuda squawked in alarm.

'Fight it, My Lord. Fight it!' cried the King of the Birds urgently. 'Fight your hunger and your thirst now and I promise you, you shall soon have food and drink. Climb onto my back quickly and we shall be away.'

Garuda pushed its body against Krishna's, and slowly Krishna crawled onto its back. He put his arms around the great bird's neck and buried his face in the warm softness of its feathers. Krishna wept. Hot tears fell from his eyes, but he was too weak even to wipe them away.

Krishna woke up to feel air streaming over his body, and a cool comforting weightlessness. He was healed and refreshed, and he felt a satifying fullness in his stomach. He must have eaten somewhere along the way, but he couldn't remember. Now Krishna was up in the air on Garuda's back again, clinging tightly. He was stronger now and looked around curiously. Below him, further than he could imagine, passed the patchwork of green and ochre and rusty-brown which was India. Garuda was flying westwards, riding on the thermal air currents. They glided over deep blue oceans, lands of gaping barrenness, and others of dark, green forests or great, jutting, white-capped mountains. Garuda soared over them all, higher than the clouds which cosseted the tiny Earth, until the air was cold and clear and thin.

Krishna must have drifted to sleep again, for in the darkness of his dream he saw vast spirals of glowing dots and jewel-coloured planets studded with moons or ringed in rainbows. He saw pin-pricks of light which burst into brightness and then faded and died. All around him the planets and the stars and the galaxies were spinning in a graceful dance to a rhythm he could hardly hear. Gradually, a resonant humming filled his dream, and Krishna began to hear the faint strains of the Heavenly Song.

It seemed to Krishna that it was a song only he could hear. It showed him the peace, the balance and beauty of the universe around him. Then he saw the fear and harshness and death which filled the lives of mortals on Earth. A vision of Prithvi the Earth goddess appeared before him, and he heard echoes of her pleading pitifully to the gods for help. Somehow Krishna understood that it was he who had to help Prithvi, but his body twisted this way and that, trying to shake off the burden. Suddenly his dream was shattered by the piercing screams of his brothers and sisters as they were killed by their uncle, and Krishna woke up shrieking the evil tyrant's name again and again. Kans... Kans... Kans...

Garuda, the King of the Birds knew that its job was done. Krishna would never be able to forget his dream as long as he lived, and one day he would rid the world of Kans. Garuda began descending, spiralling slowly down until it felt the Earth pulling gently like a magnet at its golden wings. Warm air currents carried Krishna and his winged deliverer over the land of elephants and tigers, until Garuda cast its sharp eyes down and saw the gleaming Yamuna River winding snake-like across the land.

'Your home lies below, My Lord,' said Garuda. 'Your mother Yashoda sits weeping, wondering if she will ever see you again. Go to her, but remember your duty.'

With that, Garuda swooped down like an eagle hunting its prey.

Krishna flicked the grasping hands away and pulled Kans off his feet.

THE DEATH OF KANS

As Krishna grew older, he began to listen more carefully to the gossip and complaints around him. He had heard many fearful stories about the cruel King Kans of Mathura. Almost every child was told sooner or later that if he didn't behave himself, he would be sent away to King Kans. Many mothers who despaired of their children's disobedience and bad behaviour found that stories of evil Kans soon tamed their wild children.

Kans had tried again and again to kill Krishna. The three demons Vatasura, Bakasura and Aghasura had failed to kill him, and the child had even survived drinking poison. Kans was certain that this was the child he had feared for so long. The courtiers watched worriedly as Kans paced round and round the beautiful palace gardens, always deep in thought and becoming more and more irritable as the days passed. Soon even his most trusted advisers did not dare approach him, and everyone in the palace was quiet and watchful.

One day Kans' Chief Adviser decided to hold a meeting for all the palace advisers. They had all waited for Kans' mood to pass, and when there was no sign of this happening, the Chief Adviser decided that something had to be done. Everyone knew what, or rather who, was responsible for their King's fear and worry. They had all heard the story of Devaki's eighth child, and lately had heard many more stories of the strange blue boy called Krishna. It soon became clear to them that Kans was deeply afraid of Krishna. The advisers decided that the only way to convince Kans that he would not die at Krishna's hands was to bring Krishna to Mathura, and to kill him there before Kans' own eyes. A wrestling match, with all the young men invited would not arouse suspicion. They could deal with Krishna once he was on their territory.

The Chief Adviser thought this was such a good idea that he hurried off to tell Kans. Much to his surprise, he found that it wasn't difficult to persuade Kans. The Maharajah was willing to try anything, and they were soon busy planning the tournament. Kans sent out messengers to all the towns and villages along the Yamuna River, inviting every strong young man to the wrestling contest in Mathura.

Krishna and his friends soon learnt about the contest and decided at once to go. There were to be magnificent prizes for the winner, but more importantly, they knew that the winner of the contest would become famous throughout the land. Krishna was one of the youngest, but nobody would have dreamt of refusing to take him along. After all, Krishna had proved his strength many times over.

'I know Krishna will win the contest for us,' boasted his older brother Balram, and they all began to parade up and down the street chanting 'We will win! We will win!'

As the day of the contest dawned, Yashoda hovered anxiously around Balram and Krishna. She had tried to change her sons' minds about going to Mathura. Krishna had always managed to get himself into trouble ever since he was a small child, and Yashoda was sure that he was walking into danger again. Both the boys refused to listen to her, but Balram promised to look after his younger brother. When the time came for them to leave, the whole village came out to wish the young men luck. Soon the blessings and prayers for their safety were over, and Krishna and Balram left for Mathura with their friends, laughing and singing as they went.

Mathura was busy with people crowding towards the palace, and the drums were already beating for the beginning of the contest by the time Krishna and Balram arrived with their friends. The whole city was buzzing with excitement, and there were throngs of people everywhere. Flags and garlands of flowers hung from the balconies, and everyone was wearing their best and brightest clothes. At each street corner there were peddlers and food stalls. The women had flowers in their hair and the men were wearing turbans of every colour of the rainbow. The children laughed and chattered like parrots, squealing with excitement as they saw the royal elephants mingling in the crowds. The elephants were covered in gold and rubies, diamonds and emeralds. Sitting on their backs were the mahuts who guided the elephants through the people. They wore uniforms of scarlet and gold, and they called to the people to hurry as the contest was about to start.

The wrestling match was to be held in the main palace courtyard. There was a line of guards along all the sides of the courtyard to keep it clear for the wrestlers, but people were already pushing and jostling to get a better view. The deep, shady verandas were packed full of people, and some had even climbed up the statues and columns.

On one side of the square, servants stood with large, colourful parasols over a golden chair. There was a crimson velvet and gold footstool in front of the chair, and several small and brightly clothed servant boys were sitting all around it.

'I suppose that's where Kans will be sitting,' whispered Krishna to Balram. Just then there was a clash of cymbals and a flurry of activity as Kans strode up to the chair. His servants, courtiers and the whole crowd joined their hands in Namaskar, holding them up in greeting.

'He really is as ugly as I expected,' answered Balram.

Kans was wearing a heavy, golden crown upon his head, and in his ears and on his fingers he wore pearls and precious stones of every colour. His clothes were made of soft and glossy silk, his slippers sewn with golden thread, and yet nothing could hide his ugliness. His great black mustaches swept up like buffalo horns, and his eyebrows joined together in a thick, hairy line across his forehead. Kans' eyes were dull and yellow, and his ears were too large for his small head.

Kans settled himself in his chair and looked around him importantly. The crowd was still whispering and fidgeting, so he signalled to his musicians and the cymbals clashed again. The crowd was soon quiet and waited for Kans to speak.

'I have heard,' said Kans at last, 'that there are young men here who can fight demons and monsters. I know that there are many here who are brave and strong, and I promise them a fight to truly test their strength. Which brave man is willing to fight my wrestlers first?'

A tall, young washerman stepped forward. His muscles rippled in the sunshine and he raised his fists up for the crowd to see as he walked into the arena.

'I will fight your wrestlers,' he called confidently.

'Very well,' replied Kans with a smile as warm as a reptile's. 'You are brave indeed, but remember, this fight is to the death, and you may lose. Are you still willing to fight?'

'I am willing and more than willing,' called the washerman. He turned and waved to his friends who were cheering loudly in the crowd.

'Send in the wrestlers,' roared Kans, 'and let the contest begin!'

Two wrestlers ran out of a gateway, flexing their muscles and showing off their strength. The first wrestler was as short and wide as a bullock-cart.

'Come, O puny weakling!' he called to the washerman. 'Let us see if you are man or boy!'

The washerman ran up to the wrestler who stood with his hands on his hips, laughing scornfully. The wrestler twirled his mustaches and stamped his feet. The washerman was angry at being called a weakling and he was determined to make the wrestler regret his words. However, before he could even begin to brace himself, the wrestler pulled him up suddenly by one arm and flung him to the ground. The washerman was too surprised to do anything to protect himself, and lay totally dazed as the wrestler climbed onto his victim's shoulders. He sat there for a while, laughing and jeering at the stunned washerman. Then, without warning, he snapped the poor man's head back until he was completely still.

Krishna was horrified to see what had happened to the washerman. He was so angry that he jumped up to fight next. Balram tried to pull him back, but Krishna was unstoppable. The second wrestler Chanur saw Krishna move, and at once challenged him.

'Come on, boy,' he said, 'Let me squash you like a bluebottle fly!' Chanur was as tall and strong as a tree, and Krishna looked very small against him.

'Grab him by the hair!' yelled Balram from the crowd. All of a sudden, there was quiet as everyone waited to see what would happen. Krishna stood with his legs apart. He stared at Chanur as though willing him to make the first move. Chanur, however, was certain that he could crush Krishna, and he was in no hurry to start or finish the fight. He was enjoying the attention of the crowd, and he waited for Krishna to move first.

Suddenly Krishna leapt into action. Chanur stood bewildered as Krishna ran around him and in and out between his legs, until he was so confused that he couldn't be sure exactly where Krishna was at any time. The wrestler turned his head this way and that, trying in vain to focus on Krishna. This was exactly what Krishna had wanted, and seeing his chance, he jumped up and pulled the giant wrestler down by he hair. He twisted Chanur's long hair round and round into a rope.

'Bluebottle indeed!' thought Krishna as he began swinging Chanur around him by the hair. The huge wrestler thrashed about and tried to free himself, but soon he was whizzing around so fast that he was buzzing like a bluebottle himself! When the wrestler was only a blur in the middle of the arena, Krishna suddenly let go, and Chanur disappeared into the distance like a shooting star. A roar went up in the courtyard and Krishna sat down suddenly, amazed at his own strength!

'SILENCE!' bellowed Kans furiously as the crowd began laughing and clapping wildly. 'SILENCE!' He kicked his footstool aside and pushed his servants out of the way. He marched up to where Krishna was sitting and pulled him up roughly. 'I shall deal with you myself, you miserable, mulberry-coloured mite!' he growled as he tried to put his hands around Krishna's neck.

Krishna looked into Kans' yellow eyes and he felt himself drowning in a dark, evil dream. In a moment he saw all the cruelty which had terrified people for years. He heard the screams of the babies who had died at Kans' hands. The ghosts of all the dead crowded before his eyes, and Krishna felt the panic and despair which they had felt. He realised that only he could save the people of Mathura from such misery, and he knew what he had to do.

Suddenly, Krishna came to. Kans was grunting and stamping his feet, trying to strangle Krishna. He squeezed Krishna's throat as hard as he could but Krishna stood firm, steady as a statue. For a while, both Krishna and Kans stood perfectly still. Then without warning, Kans snapped Krishna's head back. Krishna felt a shaft of pain shoot down his spine, but at the same time he began to feel a strange tingling as a magical strength filled his arms. Krishna flicked the grasping hands away and pulled Kans off his feet. He lifted the Maharajah high above his head and threw him down with a thud which shook the ground. Kans never opened his eyes again.

When the people of Mathura saw that Kans was truly dead they began weeping and cheering at the same time.

'We are free at last!' shouted a few brave ones. Long live the blue boy! Long live Krishna!' Soon everyone was chanting, 'Kans is dead! Long live Krishna!' In their jubilation, a group of people lifted Krishna up onto their shoulders and carried him up and down the streets, singing songs of praise.

'He strung wild flowers together to make a garland for Sudama's neck, and decorated his hair with fallen feathers.

KRISHNA AND THE FRIGHTENED BOY

After Kans was killed, the people of Mathura freed Devaki and Vasudev from their prison. They released Kans' father from the dungeon under the palace and crowned him their King once again. Maharajah Ugrasen was by now a very old man, and years of living in a dark and cramped hole under the palace had made him weak and ill. He knew he had to make sure that Mathura would have an heir to take his place. Krishna was his grandchild, and the natural heir to the kingdom. Ugrasen knew that his people loved Krishna for freeing them from Kans' tyranny, and they were more than happy when he announced that Krishna would be their next King.

People from all over the kingdom came to pay Krishna their respects, and he was pampered as only a prince can be. Everywhere he turned there were servants to do his bidding. Krishna tried to accept his new life graciously, but it soon became clear to him that at heart he was still only a simple cowherd. It took more than sitting on a throne and ordering people about to make a King. All Krishna knew how to do really well was herd cows and play his flute. There might come a day when he would be expected to pass judgements on his people's quarrels and give them advice. What would he do then? The courtiers were too polite ever to say it, but Krishna could see that he couldn't serve his people as well as they deserved, because at his age he knew nothing that a young prince was expected to know. Krishna had never had a tutor and he had never been to school. He felt ignorant and stupid.

The old Maharajah watched Krishna anxiously, puzzled at his unhappiness. He questioned the servants but no-one knew what the matter was.

'Perhaps he is missing his family and friends from Vrindavan,' suggested someone.

At once, riders were dispatched to Vrindavan to fetch Nand, Yashoda and Balram to the palace. By now Krishna knew that Devaki and Vasudev were his real parents, but they were strangers to him, and Krishna was pleased to be amongst the family he knew again. Yet the weeks went by and still Krishna looked sad. Eventually, Ugrasen spoke to his grandson.

'I have watched you moping around the palace for weeks,' he said. 'What is the matter, my child? What makes you so unhappy?'

Krishna looked up in surprise. He hadn't realised that anyone might know how he felt.

'You have been so kind to me,' he replied, 'but I am not fit to be your heir. I wouldn't know what to do if anything happened to you.'

The old man nodded in understanding.

'I know how you must feel,' he said, 'but you are a kind boy, and you are good and wise beyond your years. That is what makes a good King. You love your people, and I know you will rule them justly when the time comes.'

Krishna shook his head.

'It can't be enough,' he argued. 'I can't read or write, and I know nothing about war or fighting. How will I protect our Kingdom against invaders? Isn't there anyone who can teach me all these things?'

'If that is what you really want,' smiled his grandfather, 'that is what you shall have. I know of a school, an ashram deep in the jungle, where princes and Brahmin boys are taught. Would you like to go there?'

Of course Krishna wanted to go, and Maharajah Ugrasen made arrangements for Krishna and Balram to go to the ashram at once. The two brothers put aside their silken clothes, their jewellery and their golden slippers. They left the palace barefoot, and each of them wore only a simple cloth wound around his body.

'The first thing you must understand,' reminded Ugrasen, 'is that at the ashram there is no difference between a prince and a commoner. You will all need to live together like brothers. The other boys and your teacher will be your family until you have learnt all that you need to know.'

Krishna and Balram didn't find life at the ashram as hard as some of the other boys. After all, not so very long ago they were nothing but simple villagers themselves. They grew to love their teacher, Sandipani Muni. He was like a father to them and all the boys worked hard for him. They woke up early in the morning before daybreak and worked all day until late at night. They grew their own food, sowing and weeding and watering their crops, and they learnt to make their own cloth by weaving and spinning cotton. They made and washed their own clothes, swept the ashram every day and kept it tidy. In every way, the boys lived like the very poorest people in the land, and at the end of every long, hard day, they slept on the floor of their little mud huts.

Few of the boys complained. They knew that it wouldn't do them any good. Their muni was kind, but he was also firm. They were at the ashram to learn, and they knew that they couldn't leave until their muni had taught them everything he could. The time came soon enough when the boys began to do things that they enjoyed. They learnt archery and wrestling and sword-fighting, and for a while, all they could talk about was war and fighting. Sometimes, very unwisely, a few boys picked fights with others to show off their strength, but every time the muni caught them, he stopped them with a stoney stare.

'A boy who only knows how to fight and inflict pain grows up to be a stupid man,' he reminded them. 'If you want to learn how to hurt someone, you must also know how to heal wounds.'

Each day he took a small group of boys out of the ashram clearing and deep into the jungle. He taught them about herbal medicines, how to brew poultices for wounds and potions for fevers and sickness. In the middle of the day when it was too hot to be rushing about, other boys learnt to read and write. They acted out plays and recited poetry. They meditated and learnt all the gentle arts which would make them wise and cultured men.

Not surprisingly, every boy felt homesick at some time, but few were allowed home even for holidays. The only exception was a little Brahmin boy called Sudama. He and his mother lived on the other side of the jungle. Sudama's mother was a widow and they were very poor. When Sudama was a baby, all he had needed was his mother's love and care, but as he grew older his mother began to worry. How would her son grow up without a father to teach him the ways of men? The widow tried to do her best for her son in every way. She always gave him the larger share of their food so that he would grow up to be healthy and strong. She constantly went hungry, and as the years went by she became weak and ill. She worried all the time that she might die, and who would take care of her son then?

One day as she sat weeping by her hut, a tall, bearded old man came up to her. It was Sandipani Muni. He spoke to her kindly.

'Why are you crying?' he asked.

The widow wept pitifully.

'I am all my son has in the world,' she explained as she tried to wipe away her tears. 'But I am ill, and if I die he will be all alone in the world. There is no-one else to look after him.'

The muni took pity on the poor widow.

'Don't cry,' he said. 'I promise that I will look after your son. If it will make you happy, he may come and live at my ashram at once.'

The widow smiled at him gratefully, but as soon as she realised that her son would have to live away from her, her eyes began to fill with tears once again. The muni was puzzled.

'I am only trying to help you,' he said gently.

'I know,' sobbed the widow, 'and I am truely thankful, but I don't think I could live without seeing my son every day.'

The muni thought for a while. Then he said,

'I usually expect my boys to live with me at the ashram, but in this case I think I can make an exception. Would you feel happier if he came to the ashram every morning and returned home to you each night?'

This was more than the widow had ever expected.

'May you be blessed forever!' she cried as she fell gratefully at the muni's feet.

From that day on, Sudama went to the ashram everyday. On the first morning he and his mother woke up as soon as the first birds began to sing. They washed and dressed and had their breakfast by the time the inky darkness of the night had lifted and a lilac light filled the sky. Sudama never felt safe until the morning sun rose golden in the sky and melted all the jungle shadows away.

He often lay awake at night listening to the mysterious sounds which echoed in the night. The creatures which moved around in the darkness were not ones he ever saw in the daytime, but he knew the faint hurrying, scurrying noises made by the little creatures and they were harmless enough. Sometimes, too often for Sudama's liking, he heard a slow rustle, a low moan, a deep, dry cough which froze him with fear. These were sounds only a tiger could make. The thought of the slinky, stripey beast creeping about the jungle gave Sudama nightmares. Fierce, yellow eyes stared at him in the darkness, and more than once a heavy, sharp-clawed paw shook him out of his dreams. Sudama had never met a real tiger face to face, but the creature haunted his thoughts day and night, especially when he slept.

The thought of crossing the jungle alone in the darkness before dawn filled Sudama with terror. His mother tried to make him understand that most tigers were afraid of people. She made a joke of his fear.

'Why should a tiger bother to chase a scrawny little fellow like you,' she laughed, 'when the jungle is so full of nice, fat deer to hunt?'

Sudama wasn't convinced. His eyes grew round and black with terror as he imagined a tiger with its kill, blood dripping from its mouth. His mother's face softened when she saw how frightened he really was.

'Don't worry,' she said, pulling her son close to her, 'I will walk with you to the ashram every morning, and I shall come and fetch you again in the evening. Does that make you feel better?'

Sudama nodded and smiled at last.

Each day, Sudama and his mother set off for the ashram together. The poor boy never left his mother's side throughout the journey, not even for a moment. He hardly listened as his mother chatted to him about Sandipani Muni and the ashram. He kept his eyes moving in every direction, scanning the path ahead of them, and constantly looking over his shoulder. There might be a tiger crouching behind any tree, and Sudama felt sure that if he closed his eyes even to blink, a roaring, knife-fanged animal would leap out at them. Sudama's mother left him when they reached the edge of the ashram clearing. She always waited there for him in the evening, but never went into the ashram. It was better if the other boys never found out how frightened Sudama was. If they ever did see him walking in or out of the ashram with his mother, they would make fun of him and make his life a misery.

One evening, Sudama's mother became very ill. A terrible fever burned in her weak body and she moaned in pain. Sudama sat up with his mother all night, mopping her brow and stroking her hair as she tossed and turned through the hours. As the night came to an end and his mother showed no sign of getting better, Sudama began to cry. He felt frightened and helpless. He didn't know what to do. Dare he leave his mother while she was so ill, even to get help? On the other hand if he didn't manage to find someone to help her, she might die. He took his mother's hand and began to stroke it gently. He couldn't help it but the more he thought about it, the more helpless he felt.

Suddenly, his mother's eyes opened. She looked straight at him for the first time in hours and opened her mouth to speak. She mumbled something and Sudama bent down closer trying desperately to understand what she was saying, but her voice was trembling and croaky. Slowly it became stronger. It was as if the widow knew what her son had been thinking.

'My dear,' she said, 'only Sandipani Muni can help me. He knows how to treat fevers. Won't you go to him and ask him to help me?'

'Of course I will, Mother,' replied Sudama as bravely as he could, but an icy hand of fear squeezed his throat and he choked over his words.

Sudama's mother closed her eyes and turned away for a moment.

'Oh Bhagwaan' she prayed silently. 'Help my son to be brave. Help him to make this journey safely.' The instant she thought these words, she saw the face of a young boy floating above her. The boy's face was blue and he was smiling at her. A peacock feather nestled in his hair. Suddenly it all became clear to the her. She had heard a wonderful story about a cowherd called Krishna who had fought the

84

monstrous Kaliya Nag. She had even told Sudama a little about him. If anyone was an example of bravery, Krishna was.

The widow pulled her son closer to her and whispered,

'Go to the muni, my son, but if you are frightened on the way, remember Krishna. He has magical powers. Call his name and he will take care of you.'

Sudama nodded. He didn't want to worry his mother, but he didn't think she really knew what she was saying. It didn't matter. Whatever happened to him, he would bring help to his mother.

Sudama noticed that his mother had been breathing deeply for a while now, as if her mind was at peace. He watched her closely for a few minutes but he saw that her face was clear of worries. She was asleep at last. Sudama bent down to kiss her, covered her properly with a shawl and left before he had time to change his mind.

The jungle seemed darker than ever before. The trees were dense and towered over him, shutting out the light of the dawn glow. Sudama walked quickly, taking care to make enough noise to frighten away any animals he might not have noticed. Usually when his mind wasn't on tigers, Sudama enjoyed watching the squirrels and the monkeys as they frolicked in the trees. He liked to pick flowers and berries and grasses, and sometimes when he heard a bird calling, he tried to imitate its call.

There was no time for any of that today. Sudama was in a hurry. He kept his mind on his mother lying alone in their hut, trying to shut out his fear. He walked fast for a little boy, but the sun was soon high and pouring its silken yellow rays in patches on the ground. 'I must do better than this,' he thought, lengthening his stride and swinging his arms purposefully. He didn't dare run. That might be fatal. Sudama's mother had nagged him about that ever since he was a baby toddling around their hut.

'Whenever you are in the jungle,' she had told him again and again, 'you must never, ever run. When you run, there is no time to think, no time to look ahead and see what lies in front. You might just run straight into trouble.'

Sudama knew that she was right, but even though he walked as fast as he could, he didn't seem to be getting any nearer to the ashram. He was already getting tired. By now he was panting breathlessly and his ears rang with the sound of his pounding heart. Sharp cramps chewed and tore at his legs, and his head throbbed with the effort of keeping going. Soon he was stumbling over the smallest blades of grass and tiny little stones. He knew that if he didn't stop to rest, he might never reach the ashram safely.

Sudama stopped for a while. He made sure that there was no danger lurking nearby and sat down against a tree. He leaned back gratefully against its firmness and stretched out his legs to ease the cramp. He took deep, regular breaths to steady his breathing. After a while Sudama's heart stopped thumping so wildly, and he began to listen for the normal sounds of the jungle. Was he imagining it, or had the birds really stopped singing? Just occasionally he heard a timid chirp from the trees, but there wasn't the orchestra of birdsong he usually heard. Under the deep, dark canopy of the jungle where there were just a few spots of sunlight, the world was quiet. He strained his ears trying to catch the comforting animal sounds he knew so well, but there was nothing. The silence was ominous.

Sudama peered into the thick undergrowth. Was there a pair of slanting eyes watching him? His back twitched in fright as he imagined a hungry stare. Were those stripes he saw among the sharp, spikey leaves of the bush behind him? Sudama's heart began to beat faster. He tried to get up but his legs wouldn't move. His body was stiff and he couldn't make it do anything he wanted. It was as if he was pinned down to the ground by some terrible, invisible force. Sudama panicked. He screwed up his face and closed his eyes, but as he waited for the huge, fanged jaws to grip his throat and shake him senseless, he remembered his mother's advice.

'Hare Krishna. Hare Krishna. Hare Krishna...' he chanted under his breath until there seemed to be nothing in the world except those words. His whole body, the air around him, the sky and the earth rang with the sound of those two words. Sudama's panic began to ebb away. He wasn't so frightened any more, and when nothing terrible happened, he decided it was safe enough to open his eyes.

Sudama had the biggest shock of his life. There was a pair of eyes watching him. He rubbed his own eyes to make sure that he wasn't imagining things. He wasn't. There really was a pair of eyes staring at him, but they weren't fearsome, glowing, yellow eyes. These were dark and almond-shaped and dancing with fun. Sudama's mouth opened in astonishment. He gaped as one of the eyes in front of him winked mischievously and he heard a chortling voice say,

'If you don't close your mouth soon a wasp might fly into it, and what will you do then?'

Sudama snapped his mouth shut and grinned at the blueish face looking down at him.

'Where did you come from?' he demanded.

'Oh, I was just passing by,' replied the boy sitting down next to him. 'I saw you sitting here with your eyes shut tightly as if you were waiting for the heavens to fall on top of you. What were you doing, anyway?'

'I was just having a rest,' said Sudama, looking away in case the boy read the truth in his eyes. Sudama had seen this boy at the ashram, but they weren't friends. 'What's your name?' he asked.

'It's Kahna,' said Krishna, using the nickname his friends sometimes called him by. 'I suppose you're on your way to the ashram. Come on, we'd better hurry if we don't want a search party looking for us.'

Sudama remembered his mother and leapt up at once. Krishna was already a few yards ahead and he ran to catch up.

'Aren't you scared of wandering around the jungle on your own?' he asked Krishna.

'No,' said Krishna airily. 'Most animals can smell us humans a mile off, and anyway, being scared is all in the mind.'

'I suppose so,' murmured Sudama uncertainly.

Krishna studied the little boy. He was small and thin, with a pinched, pale face.

'Don't worry,' he said sympathetically. 'When you're as big as I am, you won't be afraid of anything. All the animals will be running away from you in terror!'

Sudama smiled in relief. It didn't look as if this boy was going to make fun of him after all. However hard he tried, he knew that he wouldn't be able to hide his fear from his new friend. It might be better to admit it and hope that Kahna wouldn't tell anyone else.

'I'm glad you're here,' he said. 'I was so scared to be alone in the jungle. My mother usually comes with me, but she's ill today and I have to get some medicine for her from the muni.'

'Let's not waste time then,' said Krishna, grabbing Sudama's hand and dragging him along. 'We're nearly there. If you like, I'll take you back home, too.'

Sudama couldn't believe his luck. He squeezed Krishna's hand gratefully as they came up to the ashram. Sandipani Muni was sitting under a tree with some of the boys when Sudama ran up to him, sobbing and trying to speak at the same time. He talked so quickly that he stumbled over his words. The muni put his hand on Sudama's shoulder.

'Speak slowly, child,' he said, trying to calm Sudama. 'Tell me what is wrong with your mother.'

Sudama took a deep breath and began again more slowly this time. The muni listened patiently and when the boy was finished, he went into the jungle to gather the leaves and roots he needed to make up the medicine. When he had collected all that he needed, he boiled it all into a broth. As soon as it was ready, he poured the medicine into a small clay pitcher and gave it to Sudama.

'Warm this up when you reach home and give it all to your mother,' he told Sudama. 'Don't worry, she will soon be better.'

Sudama and Krishna set off through the jungle once again. Krishna set a brisk pace but this time Sudama forgot all about cramps in his legs, and he wasn't even thinking about tigers. Krishna made sure that his new friend didn't have time to worry about his mother, or about wild animals. He played his flute and told stories as they walked which made Sudama shout with laughter. He strung wild flowers together to make a garland for Sudama's neck, and decorated his hair with fallen feathers. Krishna pointed out the butterflies which quivered like flowers in the air, and the brightly coloured birds which flitted in the branches above them.

'There's no point in worrying about things which might never happen, especially when there are so many beautiful things around us. When was the last time anything in the jungle hurt you?' he said.

Sudama couldn't remember, and the more he thought about it, the more he realised that his friend was right. The jungle didn't feel so dark and full of danger any more, and before he knew it he was already home. Krishna stopped as soon as he saw the hut.

'I have to go now,' he said, 'but don't worry, I shall be waiting for you here in the morning. See you tomorrow.' Krishna turned and walked away. Sudama lifted his hand to wave, but Krishna's blue shape had already disappeared into the deep, green shadows.

There was no time to waste. Sudama lit a fire quickly and heated up the medicine he had brought. As soon as it was ready, he poured it into a drinking bowl and took it to his mother. It was dark in the hut, but Sudama could just make out the still form of his mother. She was asleep and he shook her gently.

'Mother,' he said softly. 'Wake up. I've brought you some medicine.' He lifted her head and cradled it in his arm as he held the medicine to her lips. Sudama whispered encouragingly to his mother as she sipped the potion. She finished it all and drifted into sleep once again. Sudama watched his mother for a little while, but when he could see that her sleep was peaceful, he lay down beside her on the floor and was soon fast asleep.

It was still dark when he woke up again. He looked around for his mother anxiously, but she was gone.

'Mother!' he cried, racing out of the hut to look for her.

'Yes, dear,' she replied from somewhere behind him.

Sudama couldn't see her, but her voice was strong again. He saw that the fire was lit, and he turned to see his mother carrying a pot of water. Sudama rushed to help her.

'If we're going to the ashram this morning,' said his mother as if nothing had happened to her, 'we'd better have our breakfast.'

'Are you quite better already?' asked Sudama incredulously.

'Yes,' answered his mother. 'I feel fighting fit and strong enough to walk through jungles and over mountains.'

Sudama was so relieved that he felt tears pricking his eyes.

'I thought you were going to die,' he said quietly.

'So did I,' replied his mother. 'Tell me, weren't you at all frightened when you were crossing the jungle by yourself?'

'I was terrified,' admitted Sudama. 'I don't know how far I got, but suddenly the jungle went very quiet and I was sure a tiger was going to get me. I was so scared that I just sat down where I was and waited for it to happen. Then I remembered what you told me. I could hardly think but I kept on calling Krishna's name.'

'Didn't he come?' asked his mother.

'No,' said Sudama, 'but a boy from the ashram turned up. He said he was just passing by, but it was a bit strange. He must have come just in time because the tiger didn't appear. Anyway, we're friends now and he's promised to walk with me every day from now on, so you can stay at home.'

'This new friend of yours must be a very brave boy,' remarked Sudama's mother. 'What's his name?'

'He's called Kahna,' said Sudama, 'and he looks like no-one you've ever seen before.'

'Is he really so strange looking?' asked his mother. 'What does he look like?'

'You won't believe this,' began Sudama, 'but he's actually blue. His skin is really blue, and for some reason he always wears a peacock feather in his hair. He also plays the flute better than anyone we know. He's really wonderful.'

'He certainly must be,' murmured his mother, remembering the stories she had heard about the blue-skinned, flute-playing cowherd and his magical powers.

What could Krishna do to help him without hurting his feelings?

KRISHNA, SUDAMA AND THE SMALL BUNDLE OF RICE

Time passed and the boys who were together at Sandipani Muni's ashram left to lead their separate lives. Like the other princes, Krishna and Balram went home to a tremendous welcome. Old Maharajah Ugrasen, Krishna's natural parents Devaki and Vasudev, as well as his foster parents Nand and Yashoda were at the palace gates to greet the two boys. The jungle was a dangerous place, and it would have been terrible if either of them had been injured or killed. Everyone was relieved to see them back safe and sound because a kingdom without an heir was a kingdom without hope.

No such welcome greeted Sudama. Of course his mother was pleased to have him back with her all day and every day, but with Sudama home all the time, it was even harder to make ends meet. As the years went by, Sudama's mother knew that she couldn't put off the task of finding a wife for her son any longer. It wasn't unusual for boys of thirteen and fourteen to be married, and probably many of Sudama's friends from the ashram already had wives. It was alright for princes, who had land and wealth aplenty to attract girls from good families, but who would let their daughter marry a poor boy like Sudama?

The widow went to Sandipani Muni for advice. When she told him why she had come, he clapped his hands with pleasure.

'I have just the answer!' he cried. 'A few days ago, a poor Brahmin man came to speak to me about a similar problem. He has a daughter who might soon be too old to find a husband, but no-one will marry her because the family is poor. Would you like me to speak to the father?'

It seemed to Sudama's mother as if every time she asked the muni for advice, he always came up with an answer. Within a few days the arrangements were made, and Sudama and the Brahmin girl were married very simply in the ashram temple. Sudama was happy. Ever since he had left the ashram he had felt quite lonely but now at last he had a companion and a friend of his own age. His new wife was a quiet girl, but as the months went by she began to feel less shy in his company. They worked side by side, clearing new land and making it ready for planting. But it would be months before they had a good crop even though the new land was fertile, and they all secretly worried that they might starve before the crop was ready for harvesting.

One evening Sudama, his wife and his mother sat around their fire together. A thin gruel of rice and water was cooking on the fire. That and a few vegetables were all that they had for their meal.

'I wonder what it would be like to be really rich,' sighed Sudama's wife.

'I know we'd never have to worry about going hungry,' replied her mother-in-law.

They both began to talk about how wonderful life might be, with servants to do everything for them, serving them delicious food and dressing them in lovely clothes. Sudama listened quietly. His heart was heavy. His mother had already grown old before her time, and he could foresee his own wife growing grey and tired in the years to come if things didn't change soon. What kind of son and husband was he that he couldn't even provide for his own family?

Sudama's wife noticed his silence and she stopped talking, suddenly realising how he might feel.

'Isn't there anyone who might help us?' she asked quietly. 'You've told me so much about your friend Krishna and I heard not long ago that he is now the Maharajah of Mathura. He must be a very powerful man. Surely he would help us if you asked him?'

'Do you really expect me to go to my friend with a begging bowl in my hand?' snapped Sudama angrily.

'No, my husband,' cried his wife, 'but if he is a true friend, he will not mind helping.'

Sudama turned away and disappeared into the jungle. He knew that he was behaving childishly. Sulking never solved anything, but he did not want to be reminded of how badly he was providing for his family. It was bad enough for him to know it himself, but how could he be expected to tell his friend about his problems?

Sudama walked quietly in the jungle. It always helped him to think. He stopped from time to time, pausing to stroke the bark of a tree or stooping to sniff at a scented flower. Everything in the jungle was dusted in glowing moonlight and every sound echoed loudly in the dark.

Sudama had stopped feeling frightened of the jungle creatures long ago, and he smiled as he remembered the terrible moment of panic before Krishna had miraculously appeared before him. Kahna indeed! It hadn't taken long for Sudama to learn that Kahna was only Krishna's nickname, and he had soon found out all about Krishna's life. He sighed. If anyone could help him, surely Krishna would. Perhaps his wife was right. He had nothing to lose by asking.

Sudama decided to leave for Mathura first thing in the morning. He rose early and was ready to leave before dawn. As he was setting out, his mother pressed a small, ragged bundle in his hand.

'Here is some cooked rice,' she told him. 'It is all we have, but you can't go to see your friend without taking something for him.'

Sudama shook his head as he looked at the little bundle.

'It might look better if I did go empty-handed.' he thought, but his mother was wiser than he. Perhaps even a tiny bundle of rice was better than nothing.

It was a long way to Mathura and Sudama spent many days travelling. He kept to himself during the day, and at night he slept under the stars in the open countryside. He was too ashamed to beg for food, and for days the only thing that passed his lips was water. By the end of his journey he was so weak, ragged and tired-looking that people turned away from him, thinking him mad. Sudama saw the look in their eyes. If perfect strangers were so disgusted by his appearance, what would his friend think when he saw him in this state? Sudama's heart told him to turn back, but his feet stumbled towards Krishna's palace as if they had a life of their own.

Soon he was standing in front of the palace gates. The guards watched him uneasily for a while. Who was this wild-eyed man? One guard picked up a stone and threw it at Sudama.

'Go on,' he shouted. 'Be off with you!'

Sudama shook his head at the guards.

'You don't understand,' he mumbled. 'I have come to see My Lord Krishna.'

'And who might you be, the Maharajah of Beggarpoor?' sniggered the other guard.

'I am his friend Sudama,' replied Sudama. He whinced as he heard the men's sneering laughter.

One guard tapped his head with one finger. The chap was obviously mad.

Sudama refused to move. He couldn't turn away now. His life depended on seeing Krishna.

'I think,' he said speaking slowly and with more confidence than he felt, 'the Maharajah will be very angry when he finds out that you have turned me away.'

Something in Sudama's voice made the guards take notice. However mad he looked, the man seemed sane enough. Anyway, he looked harmless, and he certainly was not worth losing their jobs over.

'Wait here,' said one of the guards curtly. 'I will ask if His Highness will see you.'

Krishna was at his window, watching a group of young cowherds and their cattle in the distance as they slowly made their way to the river. He was thinking wistfully of the days when he might have been one of those boys, looking forward to a whole day of messing about on the river bank. What adventures they had had! Krishna missed his friends, and although he tried not to think of her too often, he missed Radha most of all.

Life had been so simple then. All he had cared about was chasing girls, stealing butter and looking after his cows. Now he was so well guarded and cared for that he hardly ever had a moment to himself. There were servants everywhere ready to do his bidding, but there was hardly anyone that he could call a friend. Even his family was too busy with court affairs to be much company.

'What a life!' he sighed, feeling sorry for himself.

Krishna turned wearily as the guard appeared by the door. He could tell just by looking at the man's face that he had brought another problem to solve.

'What is it now?' demanded Krishna abruptly.

The guard was surprised. Krishna was usually so good-natured and friendly. He never spoke rudely to anyone, not even to the servants. Perhaps this wasn't the time to bother the Maharajah with the ragged beggar who was standing at the gates.

It irritated Krishna to see the guard dithering in front of him.

'Well?' he cried impatiently.

'My Lord,' said the guard. 'There is a man at the palace gates who says he is a friend of yours. I have tried to chase him away, but he says you will see him if I tell you that his name is Sudama.'

'Sudama?' demanded Krishna. He couldn't believe it. 'Are you sure he said Sudama?'

'Yes, My Lord,' replied the guard, expecting to be ordered out at once.

Instead, the Maharajah of Mathura rushed up to the guard and gave him an enormous hug. The guard was astonished and began to wonder if madness might be catching. He couldn't help noticing that just hearing the beggar's name had made the Maharajah act strangely. He stepped back warily, but Krishna ignored the look on his face and ran out into the sunlight, calling for his friend like a lost child looking for its mother.

Sudama heard Krishna calling long before he saw him, and now that the moment had come, he felt like running away. All the courtiers and servants had heard the commotion too. They came running out after their King, wondering what the matter was. Krishna knew that he was hardly behaving in the dignified manner expected of a Maharajah, but he didn't care.

He had spent too long cooped up with his elderly ministers, nodding as if he understood what they were saying to him. He had tried hard to be attentive and wise, but just now all he wanted was a good laugh and a gossip about old times with his friend. He couldn't wait to see Sudama, and he already had his arms open in greeting by the time he reached the palace gates.

Nothing could have prepared Krishna for what he saw. A thin, ragged boy stood before him. Krishna had forgotten how years of not having enough food to eat had kept Sudama small. Krishna wasn't much older but he towered over Sudama.

Now that they were face to face, neither knew what to say to each other. Sudama stood before Krishna, staring at the ground because he was too ashamed to look his friend in the eye; and Krishna was overcome with guilt because in all these years he had never bothered to find out how his friend had fared.

The silence was unbearable, and Sudama was just about to turn away when he felt Krishna's arms around him. Then he knew that everything was alright. They were still friends.

The courtiers watched in dismay as Krishna led the ragged boy into the palace. What could the Maharajah be thinking of? Sudama could hear the people clucking disapprovingly. He knew that he was an embarrassment to his friend, and he made up his mind to leave as soon as he could. Perhaps he shouldn't have come after all.

Krishna should have known what Sudama was feeling, but after the first shock of seeing his friend in rags, he had thought no more about it. All he wanted was for them both to be as happy as they had been at the ashram.

Sudama could see how pleased Krishna was to see him, but all he could think about was the rags that he was wearing. When he saw the beautiful clothes that Krishna and his courtiers wore, he felt himself burning with shame. Even the servants were better dressed than Sudama.

Krishna was busy organising everything to make his friend comfortable. He gave Sudama some of his own clothes to wear and as soon as Sudama was washed and dressed, they both sat down to a huge feast. Sudama had never seen so much food in his life. There were so many sweets and savouries that he didn't know where to begin. He tried to hide the little bundle his mother had given him. How could he possibly give such a paltry gift to his friend when this was the sort of food he ate everyday?

Krishna couldn't help noticing his friend's strange behaviour. He saw Sudama push something behind his back, and his curiosity overcame his good manners.

'Let's see what you have there,' he said, fumbling behind Sudama's back and fishing out the ragged bundle. He turned it over in his hands and was just about to swing it in front of Sudama when he noticed the desperate look in his friend's eyes. Krishna put the bundle down at once, but before he could say anything, Sudama had already picked it up and was undoing the knots.

'You can laugh if you like, Krishna,' said Sudama handing over the opened bundle. 'I know the rice will mean nothing to you since you are used to good food every day, but it was all I had to bring for you.'

'Why should I laugh, my friend,' replied Krishna. 'Whatever your gift, it means more to me than anything my servants could offer.' Krishna picked up a few grains of rice from the bundle and put them in his mouth. He could hear the ladies in court tittering. 'I'll teach them a lesson,' he thought angrily. He savoured the rice thoughtfully for a few moments and then offered the rest around. 'This is truly the most wonderful rice I have ever tasted,' he announced loudly. 'Would anyone care to try it?'

The ladies and gentlemen of the court knew that it would be shamefully rude to refuse. They picked at the rice, expecting it to taste as bad as it looked. It didn't. The rice had the most delicate, fragrant flavour they had ever tasted. Soon they were all singing its praise.

Sudama watched in disbelief as they ooh-ed and aah-ed over the rice. He knew very well what a poor offering it had been, but did they all have to humiliate him like this? They could pretend all they liked, but he wasn't fooled. It was more than he could stand. How could Krishna do this to him? Sudama jumped up and stalked out of the room.

Krishna ran after him.

'Don't you believe us?' he cried. 'Here, taste it yourself!'

Sudama stopped. In his heart he found it hard to believe that Krishna would really disgrace him like this. Perhaps he deserved the benefit of the doubt. Sudama ate the rice which Krishna offered him. The rice was delicious. Trust Krishna to work miracles! Somehow he always managed to make everything alright in the end. Sudama smiled gratefully at Krishna.

'You are indeed a true friend,' he said. 'For a while I really thought you were playing a cruel trick on me. I should have known that you would never do that.'

'It's certainly given those know-nothings something to think about!' said Krishna. 'Now that you've stopped being angry with me, will you stay for a while?'

Of course Sudama wanted to stay. He was as happy to see Krishna as Krishna was to see him, and he was pleased that his friend wanted him to stay. Not only that, but as anyone who has spent his life practically starving in the jungle knows, living in a palace is like a dream come true.

Sudama marvelled at the airy coolness of the marble palace with its fountains and perfumed gardens. He had spent all his life doing back-breaking work, and it was paradise to have servants to do everything for him. After a few days of feasting and talking and remembering old times with Krishna, Sudama could have forgotten what he had come for if he had really wanted to.

For a while he tried not to think about the problems he had left behind at home. Having come all this way, surely a few days here with Krishna wouldn't make a difference? He tried not to worry, but deep down, Sudama knew that he couldn't stay for much longer. He couldn't expect Krishna to do any more for him. Krishna had been more than generous to Sudama since he had arrived. How could he ask for more? Sudama worried about this as he lay alone at night. On the one hand he felt too embarrassed to ask Krishna for help, and on the other he couldn't bear to think about going back home empty-handed.

Sudama didn't know it, but Krishna spent much time worrying about this too. He had listened carefully to Sudama talking. The despair in his friend's voice had been too plain to hide. Things must really have been bad for Sudama if all he could find to wear when he came to see Krishna were rags. What could Krishna do to help him without hurting his feelings? Krishna had done well with the bundle of rice, but he knew that a few clothes and a week of feasting weren't enough to really help his friend. Even if he could give Sudama everything he needed, would he accept it? Krishna was sure that he wouldn't.

The day came when Sudama finally decided to leave Mathura.

'I would love to stay with you forever,' he said to Krishna, 'but you know that I have a wife and mother waiting for me at home. They need me with them, but if there is anything I can ever do to repay your kindness, you know that I will.'

Krishna nodded solemnly. He knew that this was the way it had to be. Sudama's place was with his family in the jungle, and his own was here in Mathura.

Sudama waved as he left the palace gates. He was sad in more ways than one. He would miss his friend very much, and now having known luxury, he really understood just how poor he was. He couldn't hope to give his family a better life on his own, and instead of taking the chance to ask for Krishna's help when he could, he had been too ashamed to speak up. He knew that his wife and mother were full of hope as they waited for him at home, and he didn't know how to face them. He could have wept.

Sudama's journey home took less time than he had expected. He was well-fed and strong now, and he walked with quick, long strides. He slowed down as he neared home. Krishna had given him gifts for his wife and mother. Those might be enough to keep them happy for a while, but Sudama knew that they would start asking him awkward questions soon enough. He wanted to prepare himself for their disappointment, but he knew that nothing he could say to them would make it better. They were expecting so much, and he had brought them nothing.

It couldn't be helped. He was home now and he could already hear his wife singing somewhere ahead. Sudama was surprised. He had never heard her singing so happily and contentedly before. He began to run. Suddenly the wild jungle that he had been pushing through was gone, and he was running through a garden full of flowers. Soon that too was gone and he came upon a huge clearing.

In the middle of this open space stood a sturdy house, with a cow and its young calf tethered beside it. There were baskets of fruit and vegetables by the door, with a clay pot full of water. It was such a wonderful sight that Sudama could hardly believe it. This was something he had dreamed about for so long. Could it really be his? He called out for his wife. He would really feel foolish if all this turned out to be someone else's!

A figure ran up to him and showered him with flowers and garlands. This was certainly not the kind of welcome Sudama had expected. Was this rosy-cheeked, glossy-haired girl really his wife? Of course she was. She led him to the doorway where his mother stood waiting for him. All the worry-lines had disappeared from her face, and her clothes were not ragged and torn. The widow laughed out aloud and hugged her son tightly.

'I knew Krishna would help us,' she said.

Sudama was speechless. All he could do was stand and stare.

He pulled at her sari as if he were hauling in an anchor, determined to rip the last shreds off her.

KRISHNA, DRAUPADI AND THE GRAIN
THAT FED THOUSANDS

Much as Krishna would have wished it, the evils of jealousy, greed and tyranny did not disappear when he killed his uncle Kans. Krishna himself eventually had to leave his beautiful city of Mathura to build a stronger fortress-city at Dwarka. In the kingdoms which spread along the Yamuna River, many kings fought to keep their thrones, brother against brother, cousin against cousin.

So it was in Hastinapur, the Kingdom of Elephants. Two families, the Kauravs and the Pandavs fought each other for years for the throne of Hastinapur. Krishna was related to both the families, who shared a great-grandfather who was once the Maharajah of Hastinapur. The rightful heirs to the kingdom were the five Pandav brothers, Yudhishtir, Bhim, Arjun and the twins, Nakul and Sahadev. Their father Pandu had been the last Maharjah of Hastinapur. Everyone knew that Yudhishtir should have been King when Pandu died, but Duryodhan, eldest of the hundred Kaurav brothers, had himself crowned King instead.

Duryodhan hated his Pandav cousins with a passion because although there were only five of the Pandavs, they were more than a match for the Kauravs. When a neighbouring Maharajah decided to hold a contest for his daughter Draupadi's hand, every young nobleman entered, hoping to win. Duryodhan had tried his luck and lost. He had wanted to marry Draupadi himself, but neither he nor any of his brothers had managed to beat Arjun, who had won the contest for his brother Yudhishtir and made them all look like fools.

Duryodhan and his brothers used every trick they could think of to try to kill the Pandavs and capture Draupadi. They set fire to the Pandav home, and when Bhim managed to save his family, they tried to poison him. When they had tried everything and failed, Duryodhan turned to his uncle Shakuni for advice. Shakuni was as cunning as a crocodile, and Duryodhan knew that he could count on his uncle to help him trap his cousins.

'Why don't we hold a game of dice,' suggested Shakuni at once. 'We'll make it known that if you lose, you will give the Pandavs the throne of Hastinapur.'

'But I don't want to do that!' cried Duryodhan, astonished that his uncle should even suggest such a thing.

'Calm down,' replied Shakuni, with a smile as wiley as a jackal's. 'That's just the bait. We want to make sure that they come to play the game, and if nothing else will bring them here, the thought of winning back Hastinapur will. All we have to do is make sure that instead of winning as they expect to, they lose everything... including Draupadi.'

As soon as Duryodhan heard Draupadi's name, he agreed to the plan at once. He had waited a long time to have Draupadi for his own, and now nothing would stop him. Within days an invitation was sent to Yudhishtir, and the five brothers gathered together to discuss whether they should go. Bhim was certain it was a trap.

'You can be sure that this game will not be as innocent as it looks,' he told his brothers, 'and I think we would be foolish to go.'

Arjun disagreed.

'You know very well that the five of us can outwit every one of our cousins,' he argued. 'Duryodhan is a cheat, but I don't think he's clever enough to get away with anything if we keep an eye on him.'

Yudhishtir clapped Arjun on the back. It was just what he had wanted to hear. Although he was a sensible man in almost every way, he had one weakness. Yudhishtir loved to gamble. He never believed that he would lose, and luckily for him, he was usually right. The thought of finally putting the Kauravs in their place and winning back the throne that was rightfully his was so tempting that Yudhishtir didn't stop to think what might happen if he lost. He swept aside Bhim's arguments impatiently.

'I can't believe that you've become such a coward,' he said to his brother, whose enormous strength and appetite for food had made him famous throughout the land.

The day of the dice game arrived and all the Pandav brothers as well as Draupadi went to Duryodhan's palace. The gambling hall was filled with men. The old ones sat puffing patiently at their hookahs. The younger men were more excited and were making a lot of noise, laughing and joking with each other. All hundred of the Kaurav brothers were there, and Duryodhan and Shakuni waited impatiently as Yudhishtir settled himself down on the floor before the dice board. Bhim, Arjun and the twins arranged themselves behind their brother, and Draupadi withdrew behind a screen with the other women, away from the curious eyes of strange men.

Yudhishtir glanced at Duryodhan, expecting him to sit opposite, ready to start the game. Duryodhan saw the look and smiled with pleasure.

'My uncle Shakuni has agreed to play for the Kaurav family,' he said smoothly.

Bhim stood up to protest at once, but Yudhishtir pulled him back down. He knew Shakuni's reputation, but by now he didn't care whom he played against, so long as he won. In any case, they were trapped in a room full of Kauravs. There were only five Pandavs and a hundred Kauravs.

Yudhishtir won the first few bets for gold and horses, but as soon as he began to feel confident, the game went against him. He lost the gold and the horses that he had already won, and in order to win them back, he began to pledge more and more of his property. First went Yudhishtir's own jewellery, and then horses, elephants, servants and land. Soon the Pandav brothers had nothing left, and the more Yudhishtir lost, the more he wanted to win everything back.

He pushed away his brothers as they tried to whisper warnings in his ear. It was as if he was driven by a madness which he couldn't control. Yudhishtir even pledged himself and all of his brothers, and before long lost them all into slavery. Now there was nothing left. Nothing except Draupadi. Duryodhan and Shakuni saw that their chance had come at last.

'The only person who can save you now is sitting behind the screen,' said Duryodhan.

'No!' cried Bhim, but Yudhishtir was deaf to his cry. He turned his head slowly to where Duryodhan was pointing, looked down for a moment, and then, silently, he nodded. Bhim leapt up in fury, but he was surrounded by armed guards and dragged away still shouting and kicking.

Behind the screen, Draupadi hardly knew what to do. She was beside herself with anger. Was she no better than a horse that Yudhishtir saw fit to gamble with her life? How could he throw her away as carelessly as he threw the dice? She wanted to run out from behind the screen and pull him away from the game, but she knew that she too would be dragged away, just like Bhim. It was too late now. The pledge was made and all Draupadi could do was wait and hope that Yudhishtir's luck would change at last.

Yudhishtir threw his dice for the last time, and as soon as the dice settled, he knew that all was lost. Suddenly the full meaning of what he had done hit him painfully. He was a fool and he had brought terrible shame upon his family. What kind of man was he to gamble with the lives of his brothers and his wife? Yudhishtir sat there with his head bowed, too ashamed to look anyone in the face.

Duryodhan had no more use for Yudhishtir or for the other Pandav brothers.

'Tie them all up,' he ordered the guards. There was no point in wasting any more time on them. Duryodhan had what he wanted now, and he commanded his brother Dushasan to fetch Draupadi from behind the screen.

Draupadi screamed and fought and clawed with her nails as Dushasan tried to capture her. The time for silence was long gone, and she knew that now there was no-one to protect her.

'If Duryodhan wants me,' she thought, 'I'm not going to make it easy for him. He might not even want me if I'm scratched and scarred and bloody.' Draupadi was usually a gentle girl, but now her anger drove her and made her strong. She punched and kicked with all her might, and if Dushasan had been a weaker man, she would have won her fight. She yelled insults at him and using all her wits, she ducked and dived, trying to get away from him.

Dushasan was not particularly quick or clever. In fact he was as dull as an ox. Unfortunately, he was also as strong as one. Try as she might, Draupadi found that she couldn't tire him, and after a while she herself began to weaken. Dushasan managed to grab her by her long hair and began to drag her towards Duryodhan. Draupadi slumped to the ground, trying to make her body too heavy even for Dushasan to move, but it was no good.

Dushasan grew fed up of struggling with Draupadi. He was angry with her for making him look so foolish, and in his anger, he yanked at Draupadi's sari and began to unravel it, undressing her. Draupadi was horrified. She called out for someone to protect her from this shame, but not a single person got up to help her. The hall was silent now, except for a low, mean chuckle which escaped from Duryodhan's mouth. Both he and his brothers had been watching the spectacle and were enjoying themselves. Draupadi could almost feel their wicked eyes upon her, and in despair she began to utter Krishna's name.

'Hare Krishna. Hare Gopala,' she cried as Dushasan spun her round and round, pulling at her sari like a string on a wooden spinning top. He played with her like a cat with a mouse, as though he wanted to break her.

The whole hall was still. Everyone's eyes were focused on the two figures of Dushasan and Draupadi. How long could this go on? Dushasan could imagine how ridiculous he looked, grappling with this woman and yards of her sari in front of all these people. He pulled at Draupadi's sari as if he were hauling in an anchor, determined to rip the last shred off her. Dushasan was puffing as he heaved and hauled at the sari, but there seemed no end to it. Enough silk had passed through his hands to clothe a hundred women. Soon the marble floor was swimming in a sea of shimmering silk, and Draupadi and Dushasan were slipping and sliding like floundering fish.

Suddenly it all stopped. Dushasan was thrashing on the floor, gasping as if he were drowning in the frothy waves of silk which swept the floor. Draupadi sat up. She felt as if she were suddenly waking from a nightmare. She searched the bank of faces which rose up along the sides of the hall, looking for the face of her saviour, but there was none. All she could see were faces flushed and grinning with embarrassment. Or was it excitement?

Not one of these people had helped her, and Draupadi felt nothing but contempt for them. She scoured their faces. Duryodhan was staring at her open-mouthed. Dushasan was lying in an exhausted heap on the floor. Everyone else was looking down, avoiding her eyes. Where were Yudhishtir and the other four? Draupadi scanned the hall, looking for even one person whose shame might force him to help her to get away from this place, but there wasn't one. Except, in the corner of her eye, she saw something blue move. Draupadi whipped around trying to catch a second glimpse but all she managed to see was a peacock feather bobbing away and out of sight.

Suddenly there was uproar in the hall. The crowd was hissing and booing at Duryodhan, and even the guards who were supposed to protect him turned away and left. Perhaps the sight of Draupadi, alone and still dignified in spite if her ordeal, made all the men realise that it was they and not Draupadi who had been dishonoured. Would they have sat there as spectators if she had been their wife or daughter?

Duryodhan made up his mind to release Draupadi and the five Pandav brothers before the crowd turned on him. Once again his plans had come to nothing. The Pandavs were always more trouble than they were worth, and the best thing now was to salvage as much as he could.

'I will allow the Pandav brothers and Draupadi to go free,' he announced to the crowd, 'but you have all seen with your own eyes that Yudhishtir has lost his wealth in a fair game. All his property now belongs to me, but I will not take him or his brothers as slaves. I will allow them to live freely in the jungle, so long as they do not set foot in Hastinapur for the next twelve years.'

Draupadi and the Pandav brothers were happy to have escaped slavery, but they began their life in the jungle with nothing but the clothes they were standing in. Somehow they managed to make themselves huts from broken branches and mud and leaves, and for food, they foraged among the wild bushes and trees. Bhim, whose worst nightmare was the thought of going hungry, tried to watch what the birds and animals ate; but sometimes things that seemed safe for the wild creatures were poisonous and made them ill for days.

One day Draupadi was lying weak and exhausted in the sun. She had been ill after eating some wild mushrooms, and had lain in the cold darkness of her hut for days. Yudhishtir and the others had gone deep into the jungle to look for food, leaving Draupadi with a bundle of berries and mushrooms. If only she hadn't eaten them. Draupadi was still shivering with a fever when she stumbled out into the sunlight. Lying in the warmth of the sun seemed to help a little, and for the first time in days, Draupadi managed to sleep from time to time.

As Draupadi lay in the healing warmth, Surya the Sun god took pity on her and decided to help her. He entered Draupadi's dream as she slept under his gaze and gave her a magic bowl.

'This bowl,' said Surya as he glowed red and golden in Draupadi's dream, 'will give you all the food you need. It will fill up with food each time it is emptied, until you, Draupadi, have eaten. Be sure that you are the last to eat each day, for after you have finished there will be no more until the next day.'

When Draupadi woke up she remembered her dream.

'I wish it were true,' she thought as she opened her eyes.

As she sat up, Draupadi's foot kicked something on the floor. She bent over to pick it up. It was a bowl, a simple crude-looking thing made of clay and looking as if a child had made it. The bowl was dusty, and Draupadi began to wipe away the dust with her fingers. In the blink of an eye, the bowl filled with food. Draupadi hadn't eaten any real food since she had arrived in the jungle, and she was so hungry that she didn't bother to think where the food had come from. She finished it all up in minutes and began to wipe the bowl clean, half-hoping that some more food would appear, but nothing happened. Draupadi cradled the bowl in her hands, and as the hunger pangs which had tortured her for so long disappeared, she began to realise that everything that had happened was just like her dream.

When Yudhishtir and his brothers returned the next day, Draupadi told them all about the magic bowl. It was such an incredible story that they all looked at her in disbelief. Bhim patted Draupadi on the head sympathetically. He knew that he imagined all kinds of things when he was desperate and hungry, so he understood exactly how Draupadi felt.

'I know how hungry you must be, Draupadi. Here,' he said, handing her a basket full of berries, 'have these. You will soon feel better.'

111

'I'm not hungry,' replied Draupadi impatiently. 'Haven't you been listening at all?' She brought the bowl to show them and began to wipe it. The bowl became full of food at once. Draupadi handed it to Bhim. 'I think perhaps you should be the first one to eat,' she said with a smile.

Bhim looked at the bowl doubtfully. He wondered if he wasn't imagining things too. Unless his own eyes were deceiving him, there certainly was some food in it. He began to eat, and as he ate a smile spread over his face. A single bowl of food wasn't usually enough to satisfy Bhim, but this time he handed the bowl back to Draupadi as soon as he had finished. He rubbed his middle in satisfaction, as one by one all his brothers had their meal from the magic bowl. Draupadi remembered what Surya had told her and waited for her own meal until they were all finished.

Later that evening, Draupadi was alone once again. The others had gone to collect more wood for their fire. The evenings were getting cold now and a fire kept them all warm, as well as keeping the wild animals away. Suddenly Draupadi heard voices. A group of holy men, sadhus, appeared out of the jungle and stopped before Draupadi.

'Our begging bowls are empty, my dear, and we are hungry,' said their leader. 'Will you give us food?'

Draupadi looked beyond the sadhu and saw that more and more of his followers were coming out of the jungle. Where would she find food for all these people?'

'I can't turn them away without food when they are hungry,' she thought. 'That would be a terrible sin.' And yet she knew that she didn't have enough food to give to one person, and certainly not to the hundreds that were appearing before her.

The sadhu misunderstood Draupadi's silence.

'We shall go down to the river to bathe first,' he said. 'That should give you enough time to prepare the food.'

'I wish it were as simple as that!' thought Draupadi in exasperation. 'Even if I did have enough food, I'd never be able to cook for all these people on my own. What does the sadhu think I am, a magician?'

Draupadi frowned as she watched the sadhus turn and leave for the river. What on earth was she going to do? She wished that she could just snap her fingers and make a huge feast appear by magic. 'That would be wonderful,' she mused, and as she thought that, Draupadi realised that there was only one person who could possibly help her. After all, he had helped her before.

'Hare Krishna. Hare Kahna. Hare Govinda,' whispered Draupadi urgently. She kept her eyes closed, hardly daring to open them in case the miracle hadn't happened. 'Hare Krishna...' she sighed.

A gentle hand touched Draupadi's head. She looked up at once. A smiling blue face was watching her. Draupadi looked into the kind eyes. She knew at once who it was and fell to Krishna's feet.

'I am hungry, my dear,' said Krishna, imitating the old sadhu's trembling voice.

This was not what Draupadi had been expecting. She began to weep in disappointment.

'My Lord,' she cried. 'I know that I will be cursed for saying so, but I have no food to give you or to the sadhus who came before you.'

'There's no need to cry, Draupadi,' said Krishna quietly. 'Bring me your bowl and I will see what I can do for you.'

Draupadi scrambled up and fetched the bowl at once. Krishna took it from her and looked at it thoughtfully. Then he put his hand in and carefully picked up a grain of rice which had stuck to the side.

'Look,' said Krishna. 'I knew there would be something for me to eat.' He held up the single grain of rice to show Draupadi and put it in his mouth. 'There!' he said in satisfaction. 'I'm certainly not hungry any more and I promise you that none of the sadhus across the land are either.'

From that day, Draupadi was certain that Krishna would be there to help her whenever she was in trouble. If she heard any of the Pandav brothers complaining about their life in the jungle, she never failed to remind him about how Krishna had helped her. As time went by, the brothers began to believe that Krishna might be their saviour too.

The years in the jungle passed slowly, but the time came at last when Draupadi and the Pandav brothers could think about returning to Hastinapur. They knew that a terrible battle with the Kauravs was inevitable if they were going to win their throne back. It would be nothing less than a battle between the forces of good and evil, and they knew that they could only win it with Krishna's help.

It was, indeed, a terrible battle, a battle in which Krishna brought all his powers of good to help the Pandavs win. But that is another story.

Book Agent

Foxwood International Sta
P.O. Box 267
145 Queen St Sou
Mississanga
Ontario
Tel (416) 567 - 98 00